MW01504091

THE GUTHRIE SHORT STORIES

BOOK 5 OF THE BEVERLEY GREEN ADVENTURES

ANDREA C. NEIL

The Guthrie Short Stories

Copyright © 2020 by Andrea C. Neil

All rights reserved.

No part of this book may be reproduced in any form or by any electronic or mechanical means, including information storage and retrieval systems, without written permission from the author, except for the use of brief quotations in a book review.

This is a work of fiction. Names, characters, places, and incidents either are the products of the author's imagination or are used fictitiously. Any resemblance to actual persons, living or dead, businesses, companies, events, or locales is entirely coincidental.

Paperback ISBN: 978-1-7334154-5-3

1631 Press, LLC.

Dedicated to my real-life pals - who have made my life so much more rich.

CONTENTS

INTRODUCTION

Welcome to Beverley Green's Guthrie! In these pages you'll find seven short stories about all your favorite characters from the Beverley Green Adventures.

My original intention was to write one story per month, January through December 2020. I got halfway through. I'm sure I'm not the only one whose plans changed this year!

On the bright side, this just means I'm not done yet, and there will be more stories coming... at some point. Till then I hope you enjoy this collection!

-ace

BOOKSTORE CONFIDENTIAL

EVERYTHING IS FINE UNTIL YOUR LANDLADY THINKS YOU ARE SELLING PORN…

I wiped the sweat from my brow and sat down on the floor in the middle of the large, echoey space that, in just a few weeks, would be my very own bookstore. I caught sight of the billions of specks of detritus illuminated by the sun coming through the tops of the windows, and promptly sneezed. I was going to have to dust. Again. I sighed dramatically and lay down on the floor, not caring that I hadn't swept yet. God only knew what the back of my NYU sweatshirt would look like when I sat up again—if I got back up at all.

Until about a month ago, I had some pretty naive ideas about what it would be like to open my own bookstore. I had focused on the image of me, smiling and dressed in fancy clothes (a clean t-shirt, jeans and Vans that didn't look like they'd seen active duty), handing out books to the adoring residents of my new adopted hometown of Guthrie, Oklahoma. This image was quickly followed by one where they all threw wads of cash at me in exchange for said books. But so far, reality was panning out a little differently.

I had forgotten about all the cleaning, painting, repairing and, uh, cleaning that had to be done before the doors ever opened. I was dirty, exhausted, hungry, and grumpy. Earlier in the day I'd smashed my thumb with a hammer. Twice. And I hadn't even gotten any books delivered yet—this was all from getting the shop itself ship-shape. Or technically, shop-shape.

The building was an historic one, which made it quaint, charming, rustic, and in this case, very, very dirty. Did I mention I was exhausted? I really just wanted to roll onto my side and take a nap right there on the antique wood-plank floor. But the first shipment of books was due in any day, and I had to get more done before they arrived. Because once they did, there would be stacks of boxes everywhere, and lots and lots of shelving and alphabetizing to do.

I was happier than I'd been in a very long time.

I closed my eyes, and almost did doze off but before I could, I heard the door to the shop open and close. I begrudgingly sat back up in time to see Kelly Passicheck, my attorney, wander in. She looked around the space in amazement.

"Wow," she said slowly, "you've made a lot of progress! Two weeks till you open, right?"

"Yes!" I said, newly bolstered by her compliment. "There's still a lot to do, but it's coming along nicely. Say, you don't know how to install a ceiling fan, do you? Oh never mind, I'm sure I can figure it out. I mean, what's the worst that could happen?"

I was pretty sure that in the next five seconds, we both had visions of the entire city block catching fire, and people running for their lives. But we pretended like we *didn't* picture that, and instead we silently prayed that I would, in fact, be able to avoid disaster while working with electricity. Kelly just shrugged and continued to look around the store.

"Is there anything wrong?" I asked her.

"No. Why would you ask that?"

"Just wondering what brings you by, is all." Kelly had helped me put together the lease for the bookstore. I'd thought it would be a good idea to get a legal brain to sign off on the deal between me and Leona Tisdale, the owner of the building. Kelly was one of the only female practicing attorneys in town, and since I didn't have any other frame of reference, I went with my gut and hired her to help me get started. She still checked in with me from time to time, but when she did, I often felt like she was going to give me bad news; like I was somehow waiting for that other shoe to drop.

"Can't I come by just to see how things are going?" She ran her index finger over an antique wooden table, and when she saw all the fine, white dust stuck to her previously pristine digit, she winced. She held her hand in front of her like it needed to be quarantined and looked around helplessly. "Have you thought of a name for the store yet?" she asked, looking at her infected hand again.

"Still the same name that's on the lease," I reminded her.

"Really?"

"Yes."

Kelly had helped me get the space rented, but she hadn't helped me name it. As we got the paperwork ready, I had trouble thinking of a name—nothing sounded right. Then when I read the lease over and it said *The Book Store* where the name should have been, I decided to leave it. I figured I'd get back to it someday. Or not. It worked fine, in my opinion.

"Okay," Kelly said in that sing-song voice that people used when they thought you were crazy. Or stupid. Time for a subject change.

"Are you sure you don't need me to sign anything? Or do I need to be in court for something? Am I being sued?" I still wanted to know why she was here. I walked over to the cash wrap and picked up the box of tissues I had there, offering her one which she gladly accepted. I made a mental note to dust that table. Again. For the third time in two days. Surely the dust would have to stop sometime.

Kelly laughed. "That's kind of over-the-top, don't you think?"

It was my turn to shrug my shoulders. She obviously didn't know me very well. I excelled in over-the-top these days—ever since I up and quit my high-payin', highfalutin' editor job in New York a few months earlier, and moved back to Oklahoma to do that proverbial Midlife Starting Over thing.

Neither of us had a chance to say anything else, however, because right then, the front door opened again. "Bev?" a manly voice called out.

"Yup!" I answered, walking toward the door. It was Mike, the UPS man. He and I had been spending a lot of quality time together over the last few weeks as I had various supplies and equipment delivered to the store.

"Got your first shipment of books in the truck," he said, jerking his thumb toward the windows. They were darkened by the kraft paper I'd hung up to keep people from seeing in, but we all looked that direction anyway, as if we had x-ray vision. "Ready?" he asked.

"Not even close!" I exclaimed. "But let's do it anyway!"

This was it. This was the moment when my dusty, bare shop turned into a bookstore. Kelly and I looked at each other, and walked to the door where Mike was waiting for us. "I've unloaded a few boxes already; we just need to bring them in," he said.

We walked out into the bright summer sunshine and I shielded my eyes as I looked toward his truck. Sure enough, there were three tall stacks of large brown boxes.

"Now we can see Mike's muscles in action," said Kelly in a low but distinctly interested voice. She was married, but that didn't mean she couldn't appreciate the fine physique of a healthy young guy who lifted boxes for a living.

"Amen, sister," I said just as quietly. I was single; I could *definitely* appreciate. We weren't weird about it or anything. We were just two very observant women appreciating nice biceps. We walked over to the stacks of boxes, and I glanced at the shipping labels of the ones on top. I had gotten books from several different distributors, including one that specialized in romance books. "Oh cool, my smut is here!" I said excitedly.

Kelly laughed, and as I looked up at her, I caught sight of a rotund, white-haired gentleman staring at me from across the street, his eyes open wide like he'd seen a ghost. He looked to be in his late sixties and was wearing a black t-shirt that said *RED WHITE & BBQ* in big white block letters. I could read it very clearly since the letters were big, and they were spread out over his equally voluminous stomach. I shook my head and refocused on the boxes in front of me.

"Let's get these inside," said Mike, tipping a stack of boxes to slide his dolly under them. Then he grunted once as he tilted the dolly back and walked the entire stack into the shop. Kelly put her hand on my arm to steady herself, and we both took in a sharp breath. And then laughed at ourselves.

Twenty minutes later, Kelly and I were standing in the middle of the shop surrounded by four tall stacks of boxes. I handed her a box knife, and we started unpacking books. Then we proceeded to take them to different places in the store and stack them on the floor in front of the shelf where they were going to go. Once everything was unpacked from the boxes, I would start arranging the books on the shelves. My store was really taking shape. Everything was happening on schedule, and everything was running smoothly. It was really happening.

The following day I celebrated a milestone in the bookstore countdown: it was exactly two weeks before The Book Store was due to open. I got an early start on the shelving, and right before lunch Mike stopped by with more boxes. I took a break to eat my brown-bag lunch in the middle of the floor of the shop, and I read while I ate. I'd unpacked *Smilla's Sense of Snow* earlier in the day and thought I'd revisit it. Not exactly a cheery book, but good nonetheless. My cell phone rang, and I answered it with a full mouth of PB and J.

"Mrphl," I said into the phone.

"Bev, it's Kelly. Listen, something's come up."

I tried to swallow my bite of sandwich, but still had a glob of peanut butter on the roof of my mouth. "Wha?"

"It's Leona. She says she doesn't want to lease her storefront to you."

"Wha?"

"I'm not sure why, or what's going on. I'll try to get more information this afternoon, okay? Just don't panic quite yet. I'll catch you later." And with that, she hung up.

Wha?

I finally got the peanut butter off the roof of my mouth and said, very loudly, "What in tarnation?" to all of the books. None of them answered. Surely I misheard Kelly when she said that my landlady had decided, two weeks before I was scheduled to open, that she didn't want to rent her building to me. Surely Kelly had misspoken when she told me not to panic *quite yet*. Surely this was all some weird dream. I looked at my sandwich and took another bite. Nope, didn't taste like a dream. This tasted real.

I had no idea what Kelly was talking about. Could my landlady even change her mind like that? Wasn't that what a contract was for? I was confused, and regardless of what she had told me, I was starting to panic. I needed a cappuccino, stat.

I stuffed some potato chips into my sandwich (this made it a viable "to-go" snack), grabbed my keys and some cash, and headed out the door. After locking up, I walked toward Hoboken, a really great coffee shop I'd discovered the week before. I ate the remaining half of my crunchy sandwich as I walked.

It was a sunny day, and being almost noon, it was starting to get hot. I usually avoided the noonday sun in the summer months, but this was a coffee emergency. I decided that when I got back to the shop, I'd call Kelly and properly ask her what in Star's Hollow she had been talking about.

Hoboken was busy, but Seth, my favorite barista, was efficient, and I soon had my delicious cappuccino to go. As I walked back to the shop, I passed by Barb's Salon, and happened to glance in the wide front windows. There was Leona Tisdale, my landlady and the party pooper who didn't want me to open up a bookstore in her stupid old building. Before my brain could say *uh, Bev, hold up a sec! Why don't you wait and let your attorney handle this?* my ego interrupted. In fact, my brain only got as far as *uh* before I found myself standing inside Barb's Salon. And just then the name *Barb* took on a whole new meaning, as I stood there with fifteen senior citizen ladies glaring at me. Some sat under hairdryers. A few were seated in barber shop chairs, and even more sat drinking coffee, waiting for their appointment. But every single person in the shop had two things in common: they were all wearing something with floral print, and they were all looking straight at me. I could feel their stares piercing my skin.

Leona was standing in the middle of the room, coffee cup in one hand, *Good Housekeeping* magazine in the other. I looked her in the eye and in that one glare, she seemed to say to me, *How dare you invade my sacred beauty space* combined with *What the heck do you want now,* and just a dash of *This better not be about money.*

"Leona," I started.

"I'm busy here, Beverley."

"But—"

"Please call to make an appointment if you want to talk to me."

"I just wanted to—"

"Doris, is that my phone ringing in my purse?"

"But the book—"

"I've got to run, dear; let's talk later, mkay?" And with that, she turned and swished to the back of the shop and hung a sharp left.

As I stood there wondering what had just happened, I could feel my face get very hot, and I began to fear for my physical well-being. I slowly looked around the room, the ladies still staring at me. I began to back slowly toward the door, worrying that if I moved too quickly, they might charge. Sweat was gathering on my forehead. I groped for the handle of the door, sidled out, and ran.

All in all, it went great.

When I got back to The Book Store, out of breath and missing most of my cappuccino because I'd spilled it as I ran, I found Kelly waiting for me at the door.

"Where have you been?" she asked impatiently. Lawyers.

"I—"

"You didn't try to talk to Leona, did you?"

"Are you clairvoyant?" I asked.

"Look, just don't talk to her directly, okay?" She ran right over my question without answering it, like she often did. She was direct and to the point, that was for sure. I could respect that, however personally annoying I found it.

"Okay," I said quietly.

"Leona thinks you are opening up a porn shop."

I dropped my coffee cup on the sidewalk. "Those are the weirdest words I've heard put together in a sentence since I left New York," I said, picking up the now-empty cup. I looked at it sadly, mourning its passing before unlocking the front door. "That doesn't even make any sense."

"Yeah, I'll admit this is a weird one," she said, following me in.

"Can she even do that?"

"I'm not sure, to be honest." She pulled a manila folder out of a stack that she'd plopped on the countertop. It was held together with a big rubber band. She snapped the rubber band off and proceeded to look through the papers.

"But you're supposed to know everything!"

She shot me a look before continuing. "There are provisions in the lease that keep either of you from canceling the contract for no good reason. But there are also provisions in the lease that keep you from selling certain things. Like, you can't change your mind and decide to open a yoga studio instead of a bookstore, without express written permission from Leona."

"Why on earth would I want to open a yoga studio?" I asked. Clearly Kelly didn't know me very well.

"That was just an example, Bev. Obviously."

"But I am also not opening a—what did you call it? A porn shop? I don't even know what that is!"

She shot me another look. "Really?"

I started to blush. "Okay fine, I can maybe imagine. But I am definitely not doing that! Why would she even think that?"

"I have no freakin' idea. But her attorney says she's threatening to terminate the lease."

"She can't do that. She's just flat-out wrong! I am not violating the terms of the lease!" I knew I was starting to sound hysterical, but it was just the weirdest thing ever and I was having a hard time wrapping my brain around it. It was as if...it was as if I was really excited to realize a dream I'd had for years, only to have someone tell me that they weren't going to let me do it. Yes, it was just like that.

"I'll work on it. In the meantime, keep setting up. I'll see if I can write them a letter explaining there's been a mix-up." Kelly snapped the rubber band back on my file, gathered up her things, and left the shop without another word. I guess I had to pay extra for sympathy.

So what now? I was feeling even more stressed, even more helpless. I couldn't focus on alphabetizing books, so I decided to call it a day.

When I got home, I grabbed an Emergency Beer from the fridge, and went out back to say hi to the girls.

The girls were the brood of chickens who lived in the coop I had constructed in my backyard when I moved in. They were eight of the cutest, fluffiest, friendliest hens you ever did see, plus one riot-inciting, ornery, anarchist bird whose name was Beryl. And she was one mean hen.

I sat down on my porch and the birds made their way over to the fence to see if I had any snacks.

"I'll bring you some treats later," I assured them, taking a sip of my beer. They clucked nervously as if they didn't believe me, and then wandered off again to look for better opportunities. Except for Beryl, who kept staring at me through the fencing. *I am coming for you,* she seemed to be saying. "I have no doubt," I said to her.

Even though chicken watching while drinking an Emergency Beer was incredibly calming and relaxing, I couldn't help but think about the trouble brewing at the bookstore. What if Leona really did succeed in thwarting my dream? It was just too ridiculous to seriously consider, but I did it anyway, because I was a professional worrier. This was not what I had in mind when I made the decision to move back home to Oklahoma. I had come back to the state and chose Guthrie as my home because I wanted a simpler, more fun life. If I'd wanted this much drama, I'd have stayed in New York.

The next few days were almost unbearable. It was just under two weeks before I was scheduled to open, and each day that went by that I didn't hear from Kelly seemed like an eternity. It was in reality only a day and a half, but still. I went ahead with unpacking boxes of books and gift items that kept arriving at the store. It was fun to put things in their place and see my shop slowly take shape; I took photos every day so I'd be able to look back at the progress. But the whole thing was dampened by a feeling of dread, like it might be taken away from me at any second. Mother Nature added her own dramatic flair to the situation by providing some spectacular summer storms, including one power outage due to lightning and two tornado warnings. She could be such a drama queen sometimes. And her timing was impeccable.

Finally, one afternoon while I was arranging books in the true crime section, I got a call from Kelly.

"What!" I yelled into the phone.

"Yes, hi," she said calmly.

I said nothing.

"Good news," she added.

"Are you sure?"

"Yes. Leona's attorney agreed that they couldn't terminate the lease without great cost of time and money. Because I assured him we would make it as difficult as possible for them to try it. And by difficult, I mean expensive."

I almost melted into a puddle on the floor. "Oh, what a relief."

"You're lucky your landlady is cheap."

Kelly went on to tell me that I should keep planning to open on the following Friday, and she would make sure things stayed quiet on the legal front. As we hung up, I felt so much more relaxed and optimistic. Of course nothing could stand in the way of me and my dreams.

The next morning was a fine, sunny Wednesday morning—nine more days until I opened my bookstore! I was so happy things were running smoothly again that I decided to take my time and walk to the shop. After packing up a lunch and checking in with the chickens, I set out for downtown.

I turned off of a small neighborhood street and onto Division Street, and as I did, a white Honda Accord pulled into an empty parking lot right in front of me. I didn't think anything of it, until the tinted driver's side window started to roll down. The part of my nervous system in charge of fight or flight had more or less been on vacation since I stopped riding the subways in Manhattan, but now it kicked right back in. My muscles tensed and I stopped in my tracks. *Alert! Alert! Scary situation!*

"Hey Bev, let's go get coffee!" Kelly poked her head out the window, smiling. My shoulders sagged and I let out my breath, which I hadn't even noticed I'd been holding.

Despite the fact she almost scared the living broccoli out of me, who was I to turn down an opportunity for coffee? Besides, a good Hoboken cappuccino sounded like a great way to start this glorious new day. I ran around to the passenger side of the car and hopped in.

But instead of driving south toward Hoboken, Kelly turned north. It turned out she had really meant "best chocolate old-fashioned donut ever, with a side of okay coffee."

"I can't believe you haven't been to Missy's before today," Kelly said as we pulled into the bakery's crowded parking lot.

"I haven't lived here long enough to know where all the good desserts are," I explained.

We went in, and Kelly ordered for us. Then we sat down at

a small table and tucked in. It really was the very best chocolate old-fashioned donut I'd ever had. It was so good it made up for the fact that it wasn't served with a cappuccino. We sat and chatted for a while. It was the first time we'd socialized outside of our business relationship, and it turned out we had more in common than I'd thought. She was a hardcore feminist and liked books, and I loved the same donuts as she did. Maybe I'd found a new friend in Guthrie.

After we leisurely sipped our coffee and unsuccessfully resisted a second round of donuts, Kelly drove me to the bookstore. She parked in a space right out front, and I began to gather up my bag to get out.

"Uh, Beverley?"

I looked at Kelly, who was staring at the front of my shop. Then I looked up and almost dropped my drink again. "What the..."

The front of The Book Store had been vandalized. Someone had painted *GO HOME CITY SILKER* across the glass windows in black spray paint. Whoever attacked the store was a crappy speller.

"Oh no, no, no..." I said, getting out of the car. Kelly got out too, and we stood in front of the windows.

"I hope the inside is okay," Kelly said.

Oh dear. I hadn't even thought of that. If the criminals had broken in as well as vandalized the outside, there was no telling what damage they could have done. I started for the door, my heart racing.

"Wait!" Kelly said sharply. "It may not be safe."

I hadn't thought of that, either. But as I crept closer to the front door, I could see that it hadn't been forced open, and when I tried the handle, it was still locked. "I'm sure it's fine," I said, not quite as confident as I sounded.

"I think we should call the police," she suggested sternly.

"Meh," I said as I unlocked the door and peeked my head in. "Everything looks fine inside."

I put my bag down inside the door, and Kelly and I stood on the sidewalk looking at the front windows. "Do you think they wanted to steal stuff though?"

"Dunno. Whoever it was probably isn't much of a reader, judging by their lack of spelling skills."

"Oh, I don't know," I shrugged. "Maybe they just had a little performance anxiety. I mean, that's a lot of letters to remember, and to get them so *big*." We stared at the uneven letters. On a few of the lower ones, the paint had dripped and made its way down the glass.

"They didn't get any paint on the actual building, just the glass," said Kelly. "Interesting."

"Yeah, they made my cleanup job easy," I said appreciatively.

"And they also knew not to damage a historic building."

"Smart hoodlums."

"Indeed."

Neither of us said anything for a while. The obvious next thing to say was *who would have done something like this?* But neither of us asked that question. Maybe it was because we already had an idea. Well, they weren't going to scare me off that easily.

"So let's just see what happens, huh?" Kelly asked.

"That's the official legal advice from my attorney?"

She shrugged.

I didn't know what to do. But if Kelly thought it was okay to move on, I guessed I thought that too.

We stared at the graffiti a little longer and then I decided it was time to get back to work, starting with scraping the paint off the windows. What a way to start the workday.

It didn't take long to get my personal love letter scraped off the glass of the front windows, and after I finished, I went inside to continue shelving books and arranging my front display tables. I wanted nice, full displays of books visible for my new customers to see as they walked in the front door. I wanted everything to be orderly, eye-catching, and irresistible. So far, so good.

Around eleven, the shop phone rang.

"The Book Store, Beverley speaking. How can I help you?"

"Is this a bookstore?" the female voice said.

"Yes, that's right! How can I help?"

"You sell books?"

I was starting to wonder if this was a prank call; an inbred cousin of the welcome message on my windows. "Yes, we will—when we open next week."

"So you don't sell...dirty things?" the voice asked timidly.

"I'm not sure I know what you mean, ma'am," I said politely yet guardedly.

"I heard this was gonna be a porn shop."

Oh dear. That was all I needed—the fine upstanding citizens of Guthrie to start spreading rumors about my bookstore. Now I had two more things to worry about: who was spreading these rumors, and what if they were successful in turning everyone against me and no one shopped at my store? Talk about a PR disaster! It would be the shortest lifespan of a bookstore in recorded history.

"Well, I'm not sure who told you that, ma'am, but this is definitely a bookstore! We will sell all kinds of books—children's books, history books, biographies, westerns...the name of my store is The Book Store, and that's exactly what I'm selling." I hoped this would do the trick.

"Mmmm," was all the voice said. "Well, I guess we will see."

"Yes, I hope you'll come to the grand opening next Friday. We'll be having some free food and giveaways! What is your name? I'll be sure to save a gift for you."

"That's all right dear, thank you." *Click.*

I took a deep breath and yelled. I yelled as loudly as I could. Which was pretty loud, as it turned out.

They say that when you do what you love, it doesn't really feel like work. Well, I don't know what idiot came up with that one, because it was so not true. Hadn't they ever heard of a "labor of love?" Yeah, sure, I didn't dread getting up in the morning anymore, like I'd begun to do in New York before I quit my fancy job. And yes, the days went quickly, and I laughed and smiled more, as a general rule. But dang. I was working long hours, and it was catching up with me.

On Friday, I arrived at the Book Store early to receive a shipment of books arriving on a special delivery truck. Still half asleep and thinking about all the upcoming physical labor, I didn't notice the front door to the shop had been pried open until I went to put my key in the deadbolt. My stomach dropped to my feet, and I backed away slowly. I couldn't hear anything inside, though, so I crept forward and slowly pushed the door open.

Books were everywhere. Everywhere except where they should have been. They were all over the floor—not stacked neatly or anything that nice. Nope, it looked like a tornado had gone through the place. All the work I'd done on my displays was ruined, and as I walked in I started to hyperventilate. I sat down on the floor next to some Oprah Book Club books, and dumped my book bag on James Patterson's face.

"Who could do this to me?" I asked Oprah.

"I don't know for sure, but I have a pretty good idea," said a woman's voice behind me.

I looked up, really hoping to see Oprah—she could save me from this mess for sure—but it was just my lawyer. I slouched in disappointment, feeling a darkness come over my soul that I just knew could only be lifted by Oprah.

"Glad to see you too," Kelly said, having noticed my disappointment at her arrival. "What in Ruth Bader Ginsburg's name happened here?"

"I'll give you three guesses," I sighed.

Kelly let go a stream of cusswords that I had never heard come out of a woman's mouth before—or a man's, for that matter. And I'd had some pretty sassy friends in New York, so this was saying something. "Did you see the windows outside?" she asked me.

I had been so lost in thought when I came in, I hadn't noticed anything amiss out front. Kelly held out her hand to me. I grabbed it and she pulled me up off the floor. We walked outside, and I inspected my front windows. Today's love message read, *GIT OUT PURVIT*.

"God bless their little illiterate hearts," I sighed. "It could be worse."

"Oh really?" Kelly asked. "This is bullshit. We are putting an end to this." She pulled out her phone, and started wandering around the sidewalk as she made some calls.

I walked back into the store and continued to feel sorry for myself.

"What the hell?" said a man's voice. My friend Mark was standing in the doorway of the shop.

"The Guthrie welcoming committee paid me a visit," I explained dryly.

"I had no idea you were so popular." He walked into the shop, looking wide-eyed at all the books on the floor. He stooped to pick one up and started reading the back cover.

"You want to buy that? Last time I checked, my credit card reader is up and running."

He looked at me and said nothing, but placed the book

down on a table. It was the only book on the table, where before had sat nice tidy stacks of new releases.

"I just came by to see what was going on over here," he said.

"Why, did you hear about the vandalism?"

"No, but I did get a really weird call right after I got to work this morning," he said. Mark was the managing editor at the local paper, the Guthrie *Ledger*. He was also my boss, because I was a reporter at the *Ledger*; I just hadn't started work yet. We had agreed I'd start once The Book Store was up and running.

"Oh yeah? What kind of weird call?"

"Someone specifically asked for me, but when Grace put the call through and I answered, they refused to give me their name."

"Man or woman?"

"Man," he said. "He told me that you were opening up some kind of shop that sold perverted pornographic material and supplies, and that I should expose you for the sex-crazed, big-city maniac you are so you'd pack up and go on back to New York City." He swept his hand in front of him, as if he were shooing me right out of town.

"Did this man know how to spell the word 'pervert?'" I asked hopefully. Mark just looked confused. I guess I couldn't blame him. "You're not going to out me to the good citizens of my new hometown, are you?"

He looked around again at all the books on the floor. "I don't see any pornographic supplies," he said. "I'm not even sure what that means, anyway."

"You could imagine," I said, then immediately blushed. Mark was a good-looking man, and from what I'd heard, recently divorced. The combination apparently made me say stupid, suggestive things. I wasn't helping the case against my own moral depravity.

"It was a weird call, and I can't figure out what their motive was. I thought I'd come down and see if you could shed any light on what's going on."

Just then Kelly came back in, putting her phone in her purse. "Okay, we're set," she said quickly. "Ben is going to come by here in about an hour, and I'll be back then too. We'll get you set up."

"What are you talking about?" I asked.

"I'm not at liberty to say, in front of *him*," she said, jerking her head toward Mark. "Client-attorney confidentiality, you understand."

Mark nodded vigorously. They'd been friends for years, so he wasn't insulted. Just curious. I was too.

Kelly and Mark left my shop, with Kelly promising she'd be back soon and then we'd get to work. But I didn't wait till she got back; I had to get started right away. I had a lot of book stacking and organizing to do, but before that, I needed to remove the *GIT OUT PURVIT* scrawl off the windows. Just as I began to lose hope of ever getting things back in order by the time I opened in a week, the truck I'd been waiting for drove up to the shop and unloaded a crap-ton more merchandise. I was so screwed.

Kelly did indeed come back in an hour, with her husband Ben in tow. I was sworn to secrecy, and we worked together to take care of a few ideas Kelly had regarding "jackass-proofing" my shop. And in the afternoon, her middle school-aged kids came by, and all of us started putting books back on the shelves. We didn't get it all done, but wc got some done, and I was so grateful for their help.

I ordered a couple of pizzas, and as the sun went down, we sat on a newly cleared patch of floor and ate together. The kids were good kids, and Kelly and Ben were obviously still very in love with each other. It was nice to see. I watched her with appreciation, and realized that she really did care about me and what happened to the shop. It was then that I knew I had a new best friend in Guthrie.

My plan was to treat myself to sleeping in on Saturday morning. You know, like normal people do. But I was wide awake at six, so I finally gave up trying to sleep and got up. I went for a run. And by run I mean I walked around the block, but I figured it still counted. When I got back, I had some good news waiting for me out in the chicken coop—breakfast! Two of the hens had laid eggs.

So far, my foray into egg production hadn't been going very well. I was chalking it up to nervous hens that didn't feel at home yet in my backyard. Or it could have been that Beryl was threatening the other hens—I could almost hear her telling her cellmates, *Give that lady breakfast and I'll cut you!*

But this morning, it was as if they'd taken pity on me and decided that I could use a nice breakfast. So I whipped up a veggie omelet and boy howdy, it was delicious.

A quick shower followed by some general tidying up around the house, and I headed out. I drove to Missy's, where I met Kelly and Ben. I always had room for donuts, so I got one, plus some coffee. We sat down to eat our dessert-breakfast, and then it was time to get going. I followed them to the shop, where we parked out front and admired the latest round of graffiti. I had thought there was no way the perpetrators could be dumb enough to come back a third time, but I had been wrong, and now I owed Kelly some donuts. The criminal's reasoning skills were about as good as their spelling; this time the message was a little more overt and obnoxious: *BEVRLUY SELLS PORN*.

"Well shoot," I lamented as we got out of our cars. No one *ever* got the spelling of my name right, even when they weren't spray painting it as wall graffiti.

Kelly snapped a picture with her phone. "I got one yesterday, too," she explained as she noticed me watching her.

"Right," Ben said sternly. "Let's see what we've got." He walked up to the front door, which was fortunately still locked this time. After inspecting the lock and surrounding area, he moved aside so I could let us all in.

As soon as we were inside, Ben headed for the computer behind the counter and logged in. Kelly and I stood near the display tables, waiting while he found what he was looking for.

"Bingo." He clicked the mouse a few more times, then held up a flash drive. "We got 'em."

"Is it who we thought?" Kelly asked, walking over to him.

"Looks like it," he answered.

"Oh heck, yeah," she said, swiping the flash drive right out of his hand. "Beverley, I'll be in touch." She turned and left the store, while Ben and I stood there, looking at each other.

"Wasn't she supposed to take you with her?" I asked.

"Yeah, but it's okay. She does this all the time when she's in the zone."

I laughed, and offered to take him home.

Later that same afternoon, Kelly and I sat next to each other in one of the booths in Stacy's Place, the local home cookin' establishment. We were waiting for two more people to arrive. Kelly had insisted we get there early, and we'd been waiting nearly twenty minutes. I really wanted to order a chicken salad sandwich because I'd been furiously shelving books all day, and was still starving even after my lunch a few hours earlier. But she wouldn't let me get any food; she said I had to wait until after the meeting. Chicken salad would be a distraction, and apparently we didn't want any distractions.

"I'm nervous," I said meekly.

"Don't worry about it," Kelly said. "Just stay quiet and let me do all the talking. Just look mean. You know, like when you would ride the subway in New York."

"Yeah, okay," I said, swaying side to side and furrowing my brow. "Yeah, mean. I can do that."

"And if I give you the signal to sign something, sign it."

"What's the signal?"

"I will give you something to sign."

"But how will I know I'm not just supposed to read what you give me?"

She sighed with exasperation. "How about I say, 'Beverley, sign this.' And hand you a pen."

I nodded. "That sounds reasonable."

Just then, our adversaries arrived and sat down in the booth across from us.

"Leona," Kelly said calmly.

Leona simply nodded at Kelly and didn't even look at me. I tried to scowl menacingly anyway.

"Kelly, what's this all about? It's Saturday. Couldn't this wait? Leona is a very busy woman." Walter Pivens, Leona's attorney, was doing all the talking for his client, too.

"We appreciate you coming by on such short notice," Kelly said.

"I would hope so! Now what's so important?" he asked.

"Leona can explain it to you," Kelly suggested. No one said anything, and Leona and Walter just stared at her. "No? Okay, I'll explain. Or actually, these photographs will explain." She slid a manila folder across the table to Walter.

Walter opened the folder and looked at the five eight-by-ten photos inside. He didn't say anything, but after he looked at the last one, he slid them over to Leona.

She barely glanced at them before shoving them back across the table. "What are these?" she snapped. "Beverley, is this some kind of porno stuff, or what?"

"Those," Kelly began, "are photographs of two people vandalizing the front of Beverley's bookstore. They also broke in the day before these photos were taken and destroyed the inside of the store. I have photos of the damage." But before she could pull out another manila folder, Leona spoke again.

"Those are just some old grainy photos of two young men," she protested.

"They are most definitely *not* young men," Kelly countered.

I looked at the photos that had been captured from the surveillance cameras Ben had set up around the front of my store. They showed two figures wearing ski masks and dark clothing. They were definitely men. One figure was thin but a little stooped, and the other was very round, with a body type that said old guy from head to toe. And the video footage had showed them shuffling around pretty slowly.

"Beverley's store is scheduled to open in less than one week. This is unacceptable." Kelly sounded stern and I was so glad she was on my side of the table.

"Well, that's just terrible," Leona said flatly. "Maybe you shouldn't open. Seems like people don't really want you here. Maybe you should take the hint."

"On the contrary, the entire community wants a local bookstore, and Beverley has received nothing but support and good wishes from everyone. Except from you. From *you,* she has received false accusations, and threats against her shop and her person. You have been accusing Beverly of running something other than a wholesome, beloved local bookstore, and you have been spreading rumors about her. And worst of all," she said, pointing to the photographs, "you have caused physical damage to your *own* property in an attempt to scare off my client. Not to mention the amount the emotional distress you have caused her." I felt her gently kick me under the table. I winced, but figured out what she wanted and tried to look really sad and tired instead of menacing. My stomach grumbled loudly, as if on cue.

Leona started to say something, but Walter put a hand on her arm to silence her. "That's ridiculous!" he said. "You have no proof of this! These pictures prove nothing!"

"Sure they do," Kelly said coolly. "Look again." She pulled one of the pictures to the center of the table, glanced at it upside down, and then put the point of her pen on a particular spot on the photo. "Right there."

Walter and Leona peered down at the photo. It was of the two men who, in a separate photo, were seen spray painting the windows of the shop. Only in this photo, they were getting into a car.

"I believe that is your client's antique car," Kelly continued. "It's the only one like it registered in the county. It's true that we can't quite prove who those two *older* gentlemen are, but we have a pretty good idea, and it wouldn't be difficult to do some fingerprinting inside of the store since I'm betting they didn't wear gloves when they pulled all the books off the shelves."

I returned to scowling as fiercely as I could at Leona, and I watched as her lips pressed into a thin, pale line. Her eyebrows knit together, and her face turned red as a ripe tomato. I tried my best not to start laughing. My scowl wavered slightly.

"I mean, how did you even come up with the ridiculous notion that she was selling porn, of all things. Why would she sell anything other than books, when we clearly stated on the lease that's what she was doing?"

Again, no one said anything. Kelly was waiting for an answer to her question. Walter got a little bug-eyed, then turned to Leona. "Is this true?" he asked her.

"Well, I don't like her and her big city ways," snapped Leona. "When I heard about what she was doing, and all her crazy sex plans... I just didn't want to be associated with her."

This time I really did start to laugh, and Kelly kicked me under the table again—harder this time.

"That, Mr. Pivens, is slander," she said. "Please advise your client to cease from uttering wild, false accusations." She glared at him from over the top of her reading glasses. "It's very simple. When Leona couldn't find a way to legally break the lease, she resorted to threats and violence. I'm sure we can all agree that this is—how can I say it—illegal. Now, I have a proposal for you. I'm sure we can settle this ourselves, and there's no reason that we need to involve the sheriff with this matter. Any more than he already is."

That was a new one to me. Had she really called the sheriff? I didn't think she had, but I wasn't sure. Either way, Kelly's statement sounded good and scary. I tried to look mean again.

And with that, the negotiating began. Kelly demanded that Leona pay the cost of hiring two people to help get my store back in order, in time to open. She demanded that Leona pay for some additional advertising over the next four weeks, and to pay for the food and drinks for my Grand Opening party. In return, we wouldn't sue Leona for slander, and we wouldn't inform the town that she had damaged her own property just because she had some stupid notion that I was selling something besides books. Reluctantly she agreed to everything, and when Kelly gave me the secret signal to sign the agreement, I did as I was instructed, and it was done.

Over the next week, I got the store all spruced up with the help of two temporary employees, courtesy of Leona's checkbook. They helped me get the books back on the shelves, and my displays back in order. Ads ran in the *Ledger,* I did a short interview on a local radio station, and the store got a final once-over from a professional cleaning crew. Snacks and drinks arrived

Friday afternoon, in time for the Grand Opening party that evening.

Earlier in the week, I had taken a gamble and hired a part-time employee for the store; I hoped that business would be good enough to support paying her for working a few days a week. Her name was Julie. She was a bookish high-school student who was good-natured and a quick learner. She also seemed to know everyone in town, a definite plus. After some last-minute training, I set her up behind the cash register at five o'clock sharp, and opened my doors to the public.

I was overwhelmed.

I was almost physically overwhelmed—there were about ten times more people waiting to get in than I'd anticipated. They all smiled as they filed in, and I heard plenty of *oohs* and *ahs* as they began to look around. The whole thing was leaving me in danger of becoming emotionally overwhelmed, too.

I tried to recover my wits, and proceeded to mill around the store for a while, saying hello to as many people as I could, and making sure everyone found the snacks. Then I stood next to the display tables and just watched. I watched the expressions on people's faces as they browsed; the little kids were so cute as they looked wide-eyed at the colorful picture books, while their parents perused the grownup books and gifts.

"Great eats, missy!" exclaimed a gruff, yet enthusiastic voice right next to me. I turned to see a round, white-haired man holding a glass of sparkling cider in one hand, and a small plate piled with hors d'oeuvres in the other.

"Thanks," I said. I wanted to ask his name, but I got distracted by his t-shirt. It was bright red, and in big white letters it said *MAKE AMERICA READ AGAIN*. Brilliant. Who was this guy? I didn't know, but I liked his shirt.

Wait. Hadn't I seen this man before? Where had that been? I seemed to remember something about an interesting t-shirt, but I couldn't quite place him. Suddenly a vision flashed in my head: a memory of unloading boxes from the UPS truck, catching a glimpse of...

But then I caught sight of Kelly and Ben coming in the front door, and she called out my name and waved at me. I smiled back, and pointed at the snacks. "There's wine behind the counter," I mouthed at her over the din of the crowd. She understood perfectly and made a beeline for the register.

Right after they walked in, Mark arrived. I watched as he looked around, his dark eyes taking everything in, like a true reporter would. Then he looked at me, and I wanted to look away because I was embarrassed getting caught watching him, but I couldn't. Our gaze locked for a few seconds, and I swore maybe I saw a little smile. Maybe.

It was a successful night. Yes, sure, I did some decent sales, but more importantly, I got to meet my fellow townspeople, and it seemed like everyone had a really good time. I could tell they still viewed me with a healthy dose of skepticism, me being an outsider and all, but I was okay with that. I knew it would take time to make friends and build trust. And I might never know how on earth Leona and her unidentified gang of senior hoodlums ever got the idea that I was opening a store of ill repute, but hopefully that was all in the past now.

I knew I wouldn't be an overnight success, but I could tell that everyone was happy to have a bookstore in town. A place where they could find adventures, and romances, and mysteries, and the history of the whole human race, told in hundreds of different voices. Stories hold our lives and communities together, and I couldn't imagine a more satisfying way to make my entrance into my new town. This was going to be fun.

BILL'S SHOP

BILL WANTS TO SELL T-SHIRTS. WHAT COULD GO WRONG?

Bill almost tripped over his man-sandals as he paced the sidewalk along Oklahoma Avenue. Sounds of traffic from the town's main drag along Division Street made him feel like he was in an urban setting, but the truth was Guthrie was a small town, past its glory days. Some had said the same about Bill—that he was past his glory days, not that he was small, because he wasn't—but that never stopped him. Guthrie would rise again, he reckoned. He looked down the street and saw someone riding a horse down by the railroad tracks. His wispy white hair floated straight up in the brisk prairie breeze.

He continued to pace but this time tripped for real. He was nervous, it was true, but as he looked down, he also noticed that the Velcro™ was wearing out on his left sandal. Maybe it was time to look around for a new pair of footwear.

But why spend all that money on new shoes, he reasoned, when he could try to fix these? Yeah, he could fix them. Velcro™ was supposed to last forever, wasn't it? He would write to the sandal company and complain about their inferior product and ask them to send him a new sandal strap. Men's size 10 wide.

Before he could get out his mini stenographer's notebook (three for a dollar at Target) to add this task to his ongoing to-do list, Leona Tisdale drove up in her Buick and parked right in front of him. Dang, but that woman looked good in a Buick, he marveled. She cut the engine and Bill stared at her fine figure as she got out of the car. Her large posterior was covered by a layer of floral-print polyester, and he knew first-hand what earthly delights were waiting under that fabric and the accompanying support hose. He forgot all about his sandal.

"You're late," Leona said tersely.

"But I've been waiting here for five minutes," Bill said, a little confused. Which wasn't unusual.

"When I came by the first time you weren't here, so I went over to Missy's to get us a snack." She held in her hand a white paper bakery bag which he knew contained two buttermilk donuts with rainbow sprinkles. Bill's eyes wandered across her floral expanse and then back to the bakery bag. He couldn't decide which was more delectable.

"Oh for heaven's sake, Bill, stop drooling and hold this while I unlock the door," she snapped, handing him the donuts. He started to open the bag, but she turned around and slapped his hand before he could. She knew him so well.

Leona unlocked the door but stopped short before opening it. "Welcome to your new T-shirt shop, Bill," she said warmly. He smiled and forgot about his sandal *and* the donuts.

A little bell tinkled lightly as she pushed the door open and they walked in. "Your security system is working," she said, as if pointing out a high-tech feature of his new shop.

They continued into the small space and Bill let out a little gasp. His dream was coming true—he was going to open his own shop selling vintage T-shirts in just a matter of weeks! And he had this cute little vixen to thank for it. That's right, Leona was not only Bill's new girlfriend, she was also now his landlady. It was never too late in life to start something new.

"What are you going to call the shop?" Leona asked as they sat on two wooden chairs near the door, eating their treats.

"I was gonna call it Bill's," Bill said.

"Bill's what?"

"Just Bill's." He popped the last bite of donut in his mouth and licked the icing off his fingers.

Leona shrugged. "Well, you might want to reconsider that," she said.

Bill snorted. "What do you know about selling T-shirts?"

"True, I've never sold T-shirts," she confessed. "I just own half the buildings on this street, plus twenty rent houses, and I run a foundation. But you got me, Bill, I've never sold old shirts."

"See!" Bill said loudly. "And they're vintage, not old," he explained. The woman just didn't get it, he thought. She sure was cute, though.

"Well, let me know the name as soon as you can—"

"I told you, it's Bill's!"

"—So I can draw up the lease agreement," she finished. This time it was Bill's turn to shrug.

They wandered around the space a little longer, making some notes about what supplies Bill would need to purchase. The shop already had a counter where he could put a cash register, and some chairs and a table, and basic shelving lined two walls. All he would need were a few tables and some of those round metal racks that held clothes hangers. He wouldn't need to remodel or even paint.

Leona handed Bill the keys to his new store and gave him a quick peck on the cheek before getting ready to leave.

"Don't forget tonight!" Bill called after her. "We have reservations for the couples floatation tank at seven!"

She waved once without turning back around, and the little bell above the door said goodbye for her.

When Bill got home from his couples floatation session with his sweetie, he pulled out his little notebook and looked over his to-do list. He had been hoping that Leona would invite him to go home with her after their float because she had much better snacks in her pantry than he had in his. But she'd insisted she wanted an evening alone, so he was left to his own devices. Which usually consisted of a tv remote and a can opener.

Bill sat at his kitchen table eating some Raviolios™ out of the can while he read over his list. He would need to drive over to Tulsa soon, to visit a shop he'd found online that sold used retail fixtures. Their website had photos of metal racks like the kind he needed, plus it looked like they had a bunch of creepy used mannequins. He didn't want to spend the money on brand new stuff, and he was sure he could find a few things in the weird little shop in Tulsa. He was going to have to ask his cousin Al if he could borrow his truck.

Just then, his cell phone, which was housed in a little canvas pouch attached to his belt, beeped loudly. It also vibrated, which caused Bill to jump out of his chair. Dang, that thing tickled! He frequently forgot he owned a cell phone, since no one called him all that often. Folks his age still preferred face-to-face contact most of the time, and he saw most everyone he wanted to see on a regular basis already.

He pulled his flip phone from its holster on his belt and snapped it open with a quick flip of his wrist. He always felt like a police detective when he did that.

"Detective Turner," he said into his phone.

No one said anything back.

He pulled the phone from his ear and looked at it. The tiny

screen said "1 new text message" in funky block letters. The kind of block letters that spelled out *BOOBIES* if you typed in the numbers 5318008 and turned the phone upside down.

After thirty seconds of navigating through the phone's menu, he finally got to the text. It was from his cousin, Al.

Al: *What's up?*

Bill hated texts. They were a waste of time and who really cared what was up, anyway? And couldn't Al just get to the dang point?

Bill: *Grlp*

He had wanted to say, *Not much, you nut job. What do you want?* But he wasn't much of a typist.

Al: *Meet me at Beverley's shop tomorrow morning at 10 and bring coffee.*

Bill loved his cousin, but sake's alive, the man could be demanding. He not only had to get up at the crack of dawn to drive the twenty minutes it took to get to The Book Store, but now he had to leave an extra five minutes early to get coffee. He didn't have time for this. But then he remembered he needed to borrow Al's truck.

Bill: *P*

He had tried for *Okay,* but Al would figure it out.

Bill rolled up to Beverley's bookstore at 10:30. Only thirty minutes late! That was pretty good, all things considered. Things like how he hadn't set his alarm, and he had to wait in line at Hoboken to order his coffee, and then he got stuck talking to Danny Cadence about organic sheep insecticide for twenty minutes.

"You're late," said Al as Bill walked into The Book Store holding a small paper cup and a brown bakery bag.

"Nuh-uh," said Bill, denying the obvious. Today he was

wearing a heather grey T-shirt, displaying a drawing of a frying pan with a fried egg falling out of it. Below the pan were the words, *OMELETTE THAT SLIDE.*

"Oh yes you are. You know you're not going to be able to do that when you got your store open. You gotta be there every morning *on time.*" Al poked his cousin in the chest with his bony index finger.

"Nah," drawled Bill. "I'm just gonna put a question mark for the opening time on the sign I hang in the front window. I prefer to think of it as a 'soft open.'"

"I'm not sure that means what you think it does," his cousin admonished. "And where's the coffee? I told you to bring coffee."

"I did," said Bill, holding up his cup. He took a sip from it before putting it down to open up his bakery bag. "And a muffin."

"Honestly, I can't believe we're related."

"What makes you think you're so much better 'n me? You don't even have a girlfriend."

Al was silent. Bill knew he had his cousin with that one and he felt pretty darn good about it. He shrugged and took a bite of his vegan apple crumble muffin. "What'd you wanna see me for?" he asked, spraying Al with muffin crumble.

Al looked around the store and located Beverley, who was shelving books in the paranormal romance section. "Beverley, can you come over here for a sec?"

Bill swore he heard her mumbling as she dropped a stack of books on the floor before joining them. "What's up, guys?" she asked as she walked over, dusting her hands off on her jeans.

"You tell me," said Bill.

Now she looked confused. "What?"

"No," said Al.

Bill turned to Al. "What, she can't tell me? What is this?"

Beverley put her hands on her hips. "Guys. Speak English." She looked toward the door. "And make it snappy."

"Oh my god," mumbled Bill. "You," he said loudly, pointing at her. "Tell," he continued, making a beak shape with the tips of four fingers touching his thumb and then opening and closing the beak. "ME." He jammed a thumb in his chest.

Al punched him in the arm. "It was me what asked you to be here, so shut up, old man, and listen." He turned to Beverley. "Beverley, would you please tell Bill that it's a bad idea to open up his T-shirt shop? He'll never sell enough shirts to stay in business. I mean, he hasn't even set up his sales tax permit and stuff like that there."

"I have too!" yelled Bill. "I did it yesterday. I looked it up on the Google. Plus, I got me a lawyer and everything!"

Al's jaw dropped and he said nothing.

"Well, that's a good start," said Beverley. "And Al, Bill has asked me for some help. I don't have a lot of free time right now, but I said I'd give him a hand setting up and show him the sales software I use."

"But..." Al shuffled from foot to foot.

Bill shoved the rest of his vegan muffin in his mouth. Oh so good. "It'll be fine, Al. Stop worryin'! Besides, my sweetie buns will take care of me."

"What, you mean Beverley here?" asked Al, confused.

"Oh my god, no," said Beverley, her eyes widening in fear.

"Nuh-uh," Bill explained. "My other sweetie buns. I mean, wait. Like, my only sweetie buns. Leona sweetie buns!"

Both Al and Beverley cringed. "Please Bill, no more sweetie buns," said Beverley. Bill shrugged again.

"Bev, just tell him already!" Al was practically whining. "Tell him it's not a good idea. Tell him it's a *bad* idea."

"I can't," Beverley said. "I think it's a pretty good idea, actually. Hey Bill, did you decide on a name yet?"

"Bill's," said Bill, finishing his coffee. He was starting to feel a buzz.

"Bill's what?" asked Al.

"Just Bill's." Bill didn't have time for this idiocy.

"Are you sure you don't want the name to be a little more descriptive? I mean, you can tell right away what kind of shop this is by the name." Beverley waved her hand in front of her body like a flight attendant indicating where the emergency exits were.

"I don't think you can get more descriptive than Bill's," argued Bill.

"Oh lord," Al sighed.

Just then they all heard a buzzing sound, and Bill jumped. "Oh!" he said. "My phone!" He started to pull his phone from its holster, but it got stuck. "I love that vibrate option thingy," he mumbled as he yanked on his phone harder. "Feels pretty dang good."

"Oh gross," said Beverley, and she walked back to the paranormal romance section to continue putting books away.

Al threw up his arms in resignation and started to walk away too. As he did, his cousin's phone hit him in the back in the head.

"Sorry," said Bill. "It slipped."

Bill retrieved his phone, and after navigating through the antiquated menu system, discovered the buzz had been a reminder to meet the cable company at his new store. He announced his departure to everyone in book shop, which was Bev, Al, and Jimmy the Bookstore Turtle. "Don't worry, cuz," he said, patting Al on the back. "It'll be great! Now don't forget to be at the store at two o'clock tomorrow for your new employee orientating." And with that he turned on his heel and left.

After getting Wi-Fi set up at his shop, Bill realized he'd forgotten to ask his cousin if he could use his truck. Al had seemed quite upset for some reason, but he couldn't figure out why. Something to do with the shop maybe, but what could it be? Oh well. He pulled out his phone to send Al a text.

Bill: *Wan git dinr? Stacy's, 4:30*

He realized 4:30 was a little late for dinner, but it was the earliest he could manage, because he had a few things to get done before then. A few minutes later, Al answered.

Al: *OK but its gotta be at 4. Don't be late, you dumbsh*

Bill wasn't sure what a *dumbsh* was, but he intended to ask Al about it, as it didn't sound very flattering, whatever it was.

Bill: *okee dokeee*

It would be tight, but he could probably get his errands done in time.

Bill drove his Prius home for lunch, which consisted of a baloney and Miracle Whip™ sandwich on white and a can of mandarin orange slices, since his doctor told him (quite sternly) that he needed more fruits. Next on his to-do list was a trip to his storage unit, where he kept most of his T-shirt stash. He loaded up his Prius to the brim with shirts, and was surprised to find it held a lot more than he thought it would; almost an eighth of his collection. He could hardly see out the rear-view mirror. As he drove down the highway, he thought about what would happen if he crashed. The road would be littered with Dolly Parton tour T-shirts, Sponge Bob© T-shirts, and everything else under the sea including his prized mid-1990s Sesame Street™ collection. It would be a cotton-polyester blend explosion.

Fortunately, he made it to his new store safe and sound and unloaded his shirts. Which always took longer than throwing them into the car did. He tossed them haphazardly on the one table he had, and the counter. Next, he found the can of paint and the brush he'd stashed in a corner and walked outside where he painted the word *BILL'S* on his front window. He was quite proud of the fact that the letters were straight across on the bottom, parallel with the windowsill. However, when he stepped back, he noticed that the tops of each letter were *not* straight. Oh well, he thought. It added small-town charm. And there was no way he was going to pay someone to do what he could do perfectly well himself.

He went back inside and began to organize his shirts. He'd been trying to think about how he should group them. Should he have all the concert shirts together? Should he keep similar sizes together? All of that sounded like too much work. He settled for simply folding them neatly for now.

The security system attached to his front door tinkled gently, and he looked up to see his friend Marty standing at the front of the shop. Everyone called him Short Marty, on account of he was so tall. Bill found that too long of a name.

"Hiya, Shorty!" Bill greeted his pal.

"Hiya, Bill," Short Marty said. "This your store?"

"That's what the sign says, don't it?"

Short Marty nodded. "What're you selling? You got beer?"

"Nah, no beer. Shirts!" He held up an Earth, Wind & Fire beauty. Looking at it, he placed it to the side as one he wanted to keep.

Short Marty nodded again, his hands in his pockets. He looked around at the empty store. "So, what kind of beer you got?"

"No beer! Shirts!" Bill held up the Dolly Parton baseball jersey, size medium.

"Oh, you got you a concert venue!" Short Marty said, his eyes lighting up. "Where's the beer?"

"Dangit, old man, no beer! Shirts! Shirts!" Bill flapped his arms in frustration.

Short Marty's tall, lanky frame deflated a few inches as he

realized there was no beer anywhere in Bill's store. He sighed heavily, turned on his heel, and walked toward the door.

"Come back in two weeks for the grand opening and your chance to win a new ballpoint pen!" Bill called after him. Marty just raised one arm in acknowledgement. "See you tomorrow at Target!" he added. The two of them had a standing Thursday morning bro-date at Target, to peruse the new items in the super-cheap-and-useless-items section. Marty raised his arm again, opened the door, and was gone.

Bill was only twenty minutes late for his dinner date with Al. Pretty good, all things considered. Al was waiting for him with a smug smile on his face.

"What?" asked Bill, sliding into the booth and making a loud, squeaky, farty noise.

Al laughed and Bill turned red.

"I got you," Al said, once again pointing a bony finger at his cousin. "I told you four o'clock on account of I knew you'd be late. So now we're still meeting ten minutes earlier that you originally said. Pretty smart, huh?"

Bill thought about getting out his pencil and mini steno notebook to do the math on it, but as with most things, he decided not to bother. "Whatever," he said, smiling weakly. He needed Al's truck.

"That's a nice T shirt you got on today," said Al.

Bill could tell from his cousin's tone that he was being sarcastic. "What's wrong with kitties?"

"Kinda girlie, don't you think?"

Bill looked down at his shirt. His belly was perilously close to the edge of the table; strange, he didn't remember the distance between the two being that small before. Regardless, he could still see the design on his shirt: the head of a cat wearing a space helmet. The helmet was even molded to fit the cat ears. Pretty ingenious, he thought. And *not* too girlie.

"If you don't like it, you can go and—" Again he remembered he needed to borrow Al's truck.

Al was looking at him expectantly. As in, he was expecting an expletive.

"You can go and...and...aw heck, Al, it's not a girlie shirt."

"*Girlieshirt!*" coughed Al into his hand.

It took everything Bill had to just let it go. But he did; the meditation app that Leona was making him use seemed to be working.

They had a nice dinner together, chatting about meaningless things, like the existential nature of the universe, and the Law of Attraction. ("Inspired action!" yelled Bill right before the check came.) Bill paid the bill—and made a joke about it, which his cousin had only heard about eight thousand times—and waited until they walked outside to ask his favor.

It was a beautiful spring evening, and they were feeling full and satisfied. "So, what do you want?" asked Al.

"I resent the fact you think I only asked you to dinner because I need something!" complained Bill. "But now that you mention it, can I borrow your truck?"

Two days later, they went on a road trip to Tulsa to look for store fixtures. Al wouldn't let Bill borrow his truck, citing what had happened on the one occasion he had allowed it (it involved some beer, a dented quarter panel and a trip to minor emergency). Instead, Al agreed to drive Bill himself. They spent a good couple of hours going through the fixture store, picking out things that would be helpful with displaying and selling T-shirts. Afterward, they had lunch at a diner and drove back home. It was an unremarkable trip, which Al let Bill know was a good thing.

When they pulled up in front of the shop to unload the fixtures, Short Marty was waiting outside.

"Heya, Short Marty!" said Al, slapping his buddy on the back.

Short Marty didn't say anything. He just watched Bill as he waddled up to the door and unlocked it.

"You're just in time to help me unload," said Bill.

They all walked in the store, Bill with a box of hangers and Al with a female mannequin tucked under one arm. He had wanted to take it home, but Bill said no, because he needed it for the store. "It'll make them tight girlie shirts look good," he'd argued. Plus, he wasn't sure Al should be alone with a female mannequin for too long.

"Where's the beer?" asked Short Marty.

"Oh for cryin' out loud, Shorty, ain't no beer," whined Bill.

"But sign out front says Bill's," countered Short Marty.

"See!" Al yelled. "That's why you need a better name for this place. Ain't no telling what kind of weirdos you'll get in here if they don't know what kinda store it is."

"Who you callin' weirdo?" asked Short Marty.

"Come on, Marty, everyone knows you're a weirdo. That's no secret," said Al.

Short Marty deflated again. "True."

"Hmm," said Bill, lost in thought. Perhaps they did have a point. He got out his to-do list and made a note to ask Beverley what she thought a good name might be. In the time it took him to make a note, Short Marty and Al had started arguing about who made the better syrup: Mrs. Butterworth or Log Cabin.

"But which one's got real maple flavoring?" asked Al.

"Depends on what you mean by the word 'flavoring,'" opined Short Marty.

"Tell ya what," suggested Bill, "you guys help me unload

this here truck and bring over the rest of my shirts, and I'll git you some beer."

Short Marty appeared thoughtful for a few seconds. "Okay," he agreed. "But I don't want none of that cheapo stuff. You get me *real* beer."

Dammit, thought Bill. "Fine," he huffed.

They all unloaded the fixtures from Al's truck and piled in the cab to drive to the storage facility. When they opened Bill's gigantic storage unit, it was empty except for one beer can.

"Beer!" yelled Short Marty, pointing at the can.

"Where the heck are my shirts!" Bill screeched, placing one hand on each cheek, *Home Alone* style. Al was silent.

Short Marty walked to the can and picked it up. "Budweiser," he determined. "Domestic swill."

Bill tried not to cry all the way home. It was hard. He called Leona when he got to his house; she had texted him earlier with what could only be described as a booty call. But he wasn't in the mood. Leona had expressed her displeasure with his decision, but he couldn't be swayed.

At the storage unit, he wanted to call the police right away, and see if they could find clues or fingerprints or maybe a ransom note he'd managed to overlook. Al tried to dissuade him, saying maybe the shirts would just "turn up" after Bill remembered where he'd put them. But Bill said that was ridiculous; he'd put them right there in the storage unit. They waited for the police, except for Short Marty, who got bored and took an Uber to Stacy's Place for dinner.

The police were unable to find a ransom note, or any trace of his shirts. Bill was despondent.

After wandering around his house for a while, Bill pulled out his phone and flicked it open. It sparked no joy this time, and he definitely didn't feel like a police detective. He dialed Beverley's number and when she answered, he could hear chickens clucking in the background.

"How did you get this number?" she said, after he informed her who he was.

"You gave it to me, back during the sheep incident," he reminded her.

"Who is that?" Bill heard a man's voice asking in the background on Beverley's end of the call.

"Who's *that*?" Bill asked her.

"None of your beeswax," she snapped.

Then Bill remembered she'd been seen cavorting around town with Sheriff Branch. "Never mind," he said in his most adolescent tone. "Beverley's dating the sheriff, Beverley's dating the sheriff!" he sang.

"I'm giving you three seconds to tell me what you want before I hang up on you," she threatened.

Bill told her what had happened and pleaded for her help. "I need you to help me name the store. But first we gotta find the shirts or I don't got a store to name," he explained.

"I get that," she said. "Come by my shop first thing in the morning, and we'll figure something out."

"Okay. Oh, and tell the sheriff I said hi and sorry about that thing last week."

She hung up on him.

Bill was at Beverley's bookstore bright and early: two hours after she opened.

"If I don't have those shirts, I don't have a shop," said Bill, slurping on a cortado from Hoboken.

"They just disappeared from your storage unit?" Beverley asked.

"Yes, ma'am."

"Strange. Did anyone else have a key to the lock you were using?"

"Huh?" asked Bill.

"Oh dear," said Beverley.

"Oh, lock! I thought you said something else. Yeah, the lock. Well, lessee, my sweetie buns has a key because I gave her a copy of every key I had on my keyring and in my junk drawer, even if I didn't know what it unlocked..." He looked lost in thought.

"Why would you do that?"

"Well, ain't that the ultimate sign of commitment in a relationship? Giving someone all your keys?"

"The ultimate sign would be giving someone the password to unlock your phone."

Bill pulled out his flip-phone and studied it. "I didn't know this thing had a password."

Beverley slapped one palm against the top of her head and took a deep breath. "Anyone else know about the storage unit?"

"Yup. Al did, and also my barber. Oh, and my other cousin Mildred, my cleaning lady, and then there's Molly at Stacy's..." He stopped to think for a second. "I guess that's a lot of people."

"Um, yeah," said Beverley in her most restrained, impatient voice. "How much money would you say those shirts were worth?"

"Oh heck, I don't know. A bunch." He finished off his coffee and tossed the empty paper cup behind Beverley's cash wrap, where it landed nowhere near her trash can. "So, what should I do?"

"Honestly, Bill, I'm just not sure." They sat in silence for a few moments until a customer came into the store, and Beverley excused herself to go help them.

Bill sat and watched Jimmy the Bookstore Turtle, who lived in a wooden manger scene at the front of the store. Jimmy was munching on some spinach leaves that someone had left in Baby Jesus' little manger bed. Baby Jesus had a spinach blanket. The turtle looked so calm, Bill observed. That dang turtle didn't have to worry about things like missed booty calls or stolen vintage T-shirts. "What should I do, Jimmy?" Bill asked.

Jimmy looked at Bill with a passive expression as he munched his spinach. Before the turtle had a chance to answer, Al walked into the store, looking very chipper. And wearing a T-shirt that said MICHAEL SCOTT 2020 on the front, in red, white, and blue lettering.

"Where'd you get that dope shirt?" asked Bill. He could have sworn he had one like it too, somewhere.

"Uh, Ebay," said Al. "Find your shirts yet?"

"No." Bill felt like crying again. "All my hopes and dreams, stolen right out of a storage unit." He sighed heavily.

"Oh now, let's look at the bright side! Maybe you'll get some insurance money. And now you have more free time!" Al looked very happy when he said this.

"You don't understand," said Bill, swinging his feet under the comfy reading chair he'd been sitting in. "With them old shirts, I felt like my life had purpose. It's important for us old people to feel like we got purpose. Otherwise our existence is a meaningless void. And everyone knows there's nothing good to eat in the meaningless void of existence."

"How about a Reuben at Stacy's?" asked Al.

"Yeah, okay." Bill stood up and stretched. "Let me just go tell Beverley I'm leaving, I don't want her to be disappointed if I just up and disappear."

"Into the meaningless void?" asked Al, snickering.

"No, to the restaurant."

Bill meandered through the bookstore, looking for Bev. He ended up at the back of the shop, and for some unknown reason, decided to poke his head into her storeroom. And what he saw nearly gave him a heart attack.

"AAAAAAAAH! AAAAAAAAH! WHAAAAAAAT!" yelled Bill.

Beverley was the first to arrive, running so fast she nearly crashed into Bill, who was blocking the doorway to her store-room. "What is it?" she asked frantically.

Bill couldn't say anything. His jaw was frozen in horror. He simply held out one round index finger and pointed to a stack of boxes in the middle of Beverley's back room. The boxes appeared to be filled with T-shirts.

"Holy crap burgers," said Beverley.

"You *witch!*" Bill hissed.

"Come on, Bill. You really think I took your shirts? I don't even know where your storage unit is. I don't have a key. I also have no motive!"

"You don't want the competition," Bill said, more loudly this time.

"Oh get real, you old bat!" she yelled.

"Al? Al! Get back here!" Bill cried. "You'll never believe this!" He pulled out his flip phone. This time he felt even more like a police detective. "I'm gonna call the police. Do you have a phone book? Hey, Al!"

Beverley and Bill stood there looking at each other, Beverley with her hands on her hips and Bill with one hand on his hip and the other holding his flip phone. It was a standoff.

"Bill. I did not steal your shirts. Someone put them here. I haven't been back here yet today—someone must have stashed them here sometime between when I closed yesterday and this morning." She gently pushed him aside so she could get past him.

"Don't you move!" He pointed his phone at her as if to shoot.

Beverley just rolled her eyes and walked past him to the back door. "Yup, just as I thought. This lock's been tampered with! Now it's time to call the authorities."

"Where's Al?" Bill asked. They walked to the front of the store. They were the only people in the shop; Al had disappeared.

"Wait a minute…" Beverley looked like she was trying to pass a kidney stone.

"You okay?" Bill asked.

"Bill, don't be a doofus. Al took your shirts." She put her hands on her hips and narrowed her eyes. "He must have managed to pry open the back door last night."

"You're crazy! He wouldn't do that. You're just getting desperate. *You* took 'em!"

"Took what?"

They both looked up to see Sheriff Branch walking into the store. They'd been so busy arguing, they hadn't heard the door open.

"Oh now, this is great," griped Bill. "You'll just take her side." He jerked his thumb toward Beverley. "This isn't fair. We can't all sleep with the sheriff, Bev."

"I'm not—we're not—jeez, Bill, just shut up!" Beverley turned bright red. The sheriff looked a little flustered too.

"What's the problem here?" Sheriff Branch asked, standing up straighter so he could tower over Bill's short round frame that much more.

They heard the front door open. "There's no problem here," said Al, walking up to them.

"There are all kinds of problems here," mumbled Beverley.

"Al! You won't believe this! Beverley stole my shirts and is sleeping with the sheriff so he'll take her side!"

"If you don't shut it right now," said the sheriff, "I will arrest you for harassment."

Bill shut his mouth.

"Al, you've got some explaining to do," said Beverley.

"What?" asked Bill. His little brain hamster was running as

fast as it could in its wheel, but it was having trouble keeping up.

"I know," said Al, looking down at his shoes. "I'm sorry. I just thought...well..."

"You took my shirts?" asked Bill.

Al nodded without looking up.

"But how come? I mean, my *shirts!*" he pleaded. "My *babies!*" He was on the verge of tears now. Dang, but he was getting emotional in his old age. Or maybe that was what love did to you, he observed. He suddenly, desperately, wanted to see his sweetie buns.

Beverley and Sheriff Branch stood next to each other with their arms folded defensively across their chests, watching the two cousins. "You two look cute together," Bill said quietly, watching them.

"Goddammit," muttered the sheriff.

"I was jealous," said Al.

"Of the sheriff?" Bill's brain hamster needed more coffee.

"No, ya old coot. I was jealous of your shirts! You've been spending so much time with your dang shirts, getting ready for your dang store, that I was afraid you wouldn't want to spend any more time with me." Al walked to one of the comfy chairs and slowly sank into it. "Existence is a meaningless void," he sighed.

"What the hell is he talking about?" asked the sheriff.

"Oh, Al!" Bill cried. "I would never leave you to face the meaningless void alone. My shirts give me purpose! You're gonna come and work with me, and together we will stuff that meaningless void chock full of vintage T-shirts!"

Al stood up as Bill ran over to him. They hugged a deep, fulfilling cousin hug. "I'm sorry," said Al. "I really do want your store to be all famous and popular and stuff."

"I know," said Bill, snuffling a little.

"Well, doesn't that just warm the cockles of your heart," said Beverley.

"Unh," said Sheriff Branch.

Three weeks later, *Ye Olde Tee Shirte Shoppe* opened to a huge crowd. Beverley had tried to talk Bill into choosing a different name for the store (or at least use a few less *e*'s), but he wanted it to sound old-timey and descriptive, and he could not be swayed. He and Al thought the name was perfect.

Al convinced Bill to put a red-haired wig on his female mannequin and then insisted everyone call her Twyla. Bill caught his cousin trying to smuggle Twyla out of the store but threatened to tell the sheriff if he tried it again.

That first day, the store experienced record sales. True, there was no record to break, so record sales had been made on the very first shirt sold, which was purchased by Beverley. It was a shirt with a picture of a chicken on it, of course. Leona brought snacks for everyone from Missy's Bakery, and Short Marty only came in three times asking for beer. It was a grand party, and everyone had a wonderful time. Especially Bill and his cousin Al.

THE GENERAL STORE

AL "THE MUMMY" TURNER'S GOT IT BAD FOR A DAME.
IS IT THE STUFF DREAMS ARE MADE OF?

Al "The Mummy" Turner let out a heavy sigh as he left the Aces and Deuces Club. It had been a rough night—heavy drinking, heavier gambling, and dames who were nothing but trouble. That Beverley girl was after him again, and he didn't like it one bit. He only had eyes for Twyla.

He was hooked like a dumb fish. Twyla's fiery red hair and lanky frame had him mesmerized. She was tall, like he was. Her hawkish nose made him feel like he was being scrutinized when she looked his way, and he liked it. She was less shapely than other dames, but what she lacked in curves she made up for in attitude.

He had his eye on Twyla all night. He watched her from behind his drum kit as he played for the house jazz band. When he was on his breaks and stood at the bar getting a little something to take the edge off, he watched her. He could have sworn she'd looked at him at least once. He was hooked, all right. But he hadn't felt ready to make his move. When Al Turner made his move, it would be a big move, he told himself.

It was tough, being caught between two women. To be the object of more than one gal's attention at once. It was the kind of thing that would make a lesser man crumble. But he was a tough cookie.

Beverley had been trying to talk to him all night. Every time he left the stage, there she was, right next to him, chatting to her girlfriend. He'd walk to the bar and while he stood surveying the room, she would walk right by him on her way to the bathroom. Always up in his business. She was a nice enough gal and all—cute, too, if you liked energetic literary types. But she was one of those fast-talking dames, and everyone knew they were as easy to handle as a chainsaw in a thunderstorm. She owned a bookstore and used big words. She was outspoken, smart, and sassy. Women like that were trouble. And despite what people said about him, trouble was not his business. He felt bad for any guy who would get mixed up with the likes of her.

Al took a deep breath of cold night air. Yeah, that was nice. But not as nice as Twyla.

Twyla had spent the evening playing cards and drinking champagne. She'd been sitting in the corner booth with The Skink, but that didn't mean anything. Everyone knew The Skink was married and that his old lady would give him what for if she ever caught him stepping out on her. Nah, Twyla couldn't have a thing for The Skink. She needed someone who was more the strong, silent type. Like Al was.

Around two in the morning, Twyla had disappeared. From behind his drum kit he had glanced the corner booth, but both she and The Skink were gone. She must have gone home, he reckoned. When the band was finished with their last set, there wasn't any reason for him to stick around either.

The cold night air nipped at the back of his neck. He pulled his fedora lower and flipped the collar of his trench coat up to shield his neck from the breeze, but he still shivered. He was cold to the bone, and it wasn't because of the weather. Suddenly he felt a sense of dread come over him. He hadn't felt something like that since...

He pulled out the book of matches he'd swiped from the club and began to light one until he remembered he'd given up smoking thirty years ago. But that didn't mean he couldn't still imagine the feel of the nicotine burning his lungs. The struggle was real. He coughed and took one step into the street but didn't get any farther because just then a car came squealing around the corner. It was heading straight toward him at its top speed, which must have been thirty miles per hour.

Al saw a man lean out of the passenger window. The man was holding a gun. He wasn't sure if the guy was aiming the piece at him or not, but why take chances? Al dove behind a parked car. As the speeding car passed him, the thug leaning out the window fired his gat at the windows of the club. He heard a woman's scream but couldn't tell where it was coming from. Then the car tore around the corner and vanished down Division Street. Al thought he had caught a glimpse of the driver as the car sped by, and two other figures in the back seat.

When he was sure the car wasn't going to return, he got up from his hiding place and ran back into the club. There was shattered glass along the front wall, but no one appeared to be hurt. Or worse.

"They took Twyla!" he heard Rocko, the manager and bartender of the Aces and Deuces, yell from behind the bar. "They done took her!"

This couldn't be. His Twyla? No.

"Who's *they*?" yelled Al. "Who took her?"

"I'm not at liberty to say!" shouted Rocko.

Al made his way to the bar and looked over the edge. Rocko was still crouched on the floor. "What the heck does that mean?"

"Bartender-broad confidentiality."

"Oh, for cryin' out loud, Rocko," Al said. He scanned the club, trying to figure out who was there and who wasn't. Beverley ran toward him and threw herself into his arms.

"Oh Al, it's just awful! I was scared outta my wits! I'm so glad you're here." She went limp in his arms.

"I don't have time for this, baby," he said, and poured her into a nearby chair. One more scan of the room. No Twyla, no Skink. His cousin, Billy "Two-Bit" Turner, had left hours ago. Something wasn't right, but the math wasn't adding up. Had it been Twyla he'd heard screaming from the back seat of the speeding car? He couldn't be sure. But one thing was for sure—his woman was in trouble and needed his help.

Al left the club, his mind racing. He had to do something. But what?

"What's cookin', Short Marty?" Al walked into Billy's Shirte Shoppe expecting to find Two-Bit behind the counter, but instead there was Short Marty, sitting on a plain wooden chair drinking a beer. It was only ten in the morning, but Short Marty started early.

"Mummy," said Short Marty, by way of a greeting. They called him Short Marty on account of he was so tall, but Al reflected that maybe it was also because the man never spoke much and when he did, he used as few words as possible.

"Where's Two-Bit?"

"Bull's-Eye General Store. New notepad."

"Well, shoot." Al needed Two-Bit's help to track down Twyla. "I'll be back. If he shows up, tell him to meet me at Stacy's."

"Unh," said Short Marty.

Al walked down the street to Stacy's Joint for a cup of joe and one of her Humongo Breakfasts. He would need his strength for this. When he walked in, he spotted Rocko sitting at the counter, working on a stack of flapjacks as high as a pint glass of beer. Al joined him.

"What'll it be?" asked Molly, the waitress on duty behind the counter. She set a mug of hot, fresh coffee in front of him and pulled a pencil from her hair. She licked the lead before starting to scratch on her order pad. He found the gesture both mildly suggestive and repulsive all at once.

"The Humongo," said Al. "Extra cheese, no butter."

Molly wrote down his order, nodded, and left without saying a word.

Al took a slug from his mug. "That's a damn good cuppa joe," he mumbled. It really hit the spot, like a slap to the face. Strong, surprising, and a little bit scary.

"I hear you're going looking for Twyla," said Rocko with a mouthful of syrupy carbs.

"I might be," said Al.

"Might be what?" said a voice, only it wasn't Rocko's voice. It was a woman's voice. Cripes. Beverley. Al swiveled around on his stool to face her. She looked good, he had to hand it to her. She was wearing a dress that accentuated her narrow waist, and her high heels made her legs look long. Usually she looked kind of twerpy, he thought. But wouldn't you know it, sometimes she cleaned up pretty good. Today her curly hair was pinned up, revealing a feminine jawline. Perhaps a little too feminine for his taste. His thoughts went to his Twyla's perfectly androgynous features.

"Might be what, Al?" Her repeated question pulled him from his reverie.

"Look, honey," he said to her. "You're sweet and all, but I don't have time for your games. You're just going to have to face facts: I'm not into you."

"What are you talking about?" asked Beverley.

"Who's into what?" said another voice. This one was deep and masculine. Sheriff Callan Branch's head appeared behind Beverley's.

"Al's—" started Beverley, but Al cut her off.

"Hungry and wants his breakfast," he finished for her.

Sheriff Branch looked skeptical. He was a tall man; he towered over Beverley and made Al feel like a four-year old sitting in a booster seat. Suddenly the sheriff moved and sat down on the empty stool to his left. Rocko was still to his right, and Al was starting to feel a little claustrophobic. How come he felt like he'd done something wrong every time Sheriff Branch paid him some attention? The coppers made everyone feel guilty. He couldn't imagine being married to someone who made him feel guilty all the time. Wait a minute... Yes, he could.

The sheriff cocked his head at Al. "I hear you're looking for trouble."

"I'm just lookin' for a girl," said Al slowly.

"Same thing," said the sheriff. Al wasn't sure what to make of that, but he never had a chance to ask.

"You gonna order anything?" Molly asked the sheriff.

"Not right now, Molly." Sheriff Branch eyed Al while he rolled one end of his mustachio with two fingers.

Rocko didn't look up; he just sat hunched over his plate. He'd finished his breakfast but was pretending to still be eating invisible flapjacks.

"What is this, a convention? I'm just tryin' to get some grub in peace," said Al. One of the last things he wanted was a scene, and the very last thing he wanted was the sheriff poking his nose around in something that was way over his pay grade. Sure, he was the local law, but he couldn't law his way out of a paper bag, thought Al.

Everyone was silent for a moment; the air was filled with the *clink-clink* of dishes and the *rhubarb-rhubarb* of hushed conversation from throughout the restaurant.

Finally, Sheriff Branch moved. All six-plus feet of his frame unfolded from the stool and he glared down at Al. "You just watch yourself, Al Turner."

"Why, what's Al done now?" This time it was Two-Bit's

voice. Two-Bit leaned over the counter, inserting himself between Al and the sheriff. He looked at Al. "Hey, can we get a table or something?"

"I was just leaving," said Sheriff Branch. He turned to Beverley. "Could I buy you breakfast this morning?" He wore a lukewarm passive look on his face. She glanced at Al, who just shrugged and turned back around in his chair. Better to let them down quick, in his experience.

"Well," she said. "I suppose that would be all right."

The sheriff nodded once. "Let's go get us a table." He put his arm around Beverley and started to lead her farther into the restaurant. "Oh, and Mumsy?" he called over his shoulder. "I've got my eye on you."

"It's Mummy!" yelled Two-Bit as he sat down in the seat just vacated by the sheriff.

Whatever, thought Al. He was just glad Beverley was out of his hair. He didn't need some dame making eyes at him all the time. Yet he felt inexplicably sad.

However, there was no time to sit around and think about feelings, Al admonished himself. He was a man of action, and now was his time to act.

"What'd I miss?" asked Two-Bit.

"Everything," said Al.

"Jeez, Al, you don't gotta be such a wise guy all of the time. Hey, Molly, hows about a menu?"

As Two-Bit chatted to the fry cook about the high price of quality footwear, Al got back to business. "So what was with the hullaballo at the club?" he asked Rocko.

"They took Twyla," said Rocko.

"So you said."

"What, you think I'm lyin'?"

"Cool your jets, Rocko; no one's accusing you of anything." Al lowered his voice. "What was with the gunfire?"

"I dunno, Mum. I guess they was trigger-happy about it."

"Look here, Rocko, if you know anything, you gotta spill the beans, you hear me? And I mean *now*." His scowl was replaced by a wan smile as Molly placed a huge plate of food in front of him. Scrambled eggs with cheese, bacon, sausage, hash browns, and wheat toast with no butter because he was watching his cholesterol.

Rocko put his fork down. "I might have some information," he whispered. "But it ain't free, if you know what I mean."

Al sighed and dropped his head. Everybody wanted something. Everybody had their price. It was sad. What happened to the good old days, when people were more interested in creating community, and focusing on family values and self-introspection? The world was going to shit.

Al took a bite of bacon. It was so good he almost experienced a religious conversion. "Okay," he said after a few more bites. He turned to Rocko. "What do you want?"

"The usual. Twice a week for a month."

"Jeezus, Rocko." The man was insatiable, thought Al.

"You know how this works," said Rocko with just a hint of malice in his voice. "Lemme have it, or no dice."

"Fine," snapped Al. "I'll have fresh flowers delivered to the club twice a week for a month."

Rocko nodded. "Makes the place smell nice," he mumbled. "Color therapy."

"What's color therapy? Aw jeez. Never mind," said Al.

"Make sure there's some daisies in there. Those are my favorite."

"Whatever."

By this time, Two-Bit had resumed eavesdropping and was watching them expectantly.

"So spill the beans already," commanded Al.

Rocko leaned in close. "Word on the street is that Twyla owes money to The Skink."

"No!" marveled Two-Bit. He put his elbow on the counter and his chin in his hand.

Al ignored his cousin and thought hard. If his gal owed a thug some money, there was a fair chance said thug had something to do with her disappearance. It sounded plausible, and he gave himself a mental pat on the back. He could always fall back on being a private eye, if the jazz thing didn't take.

"Where does The Skink hang out, besides Aces and Deuces?" Al asked Rocko.

"That might cost you extra," said Rocko.

"You're a dirty rat," growled Al. "But fine. Fresh flowers for six weeks. And that's it!"

"The Skink's latest secret hideout is in Paris."

"If it's so secret, how do you know where it is?" asked Two-Bit.

Rocko looked down at his clean plate but didn't say anything.

"There's no time for superfluous questioning," Al said to his cousin.

"Okay, but—"

"Just shut yer yap, Bill."

Rocko got up from his stool. "I'll expect my first delivery this afternoon." And with that, he left.

"He's nice," said Two-Bit as his breakfast arrived: a hamburger with hash browns instead of French fries.

"Hurry up and eat," said Al. "We got to catch us a skink."

It took Al an hour to get his cousin into the car. First he had to get gas, so they could leave with a full tank. Two-Bit tried to get his old lady to come over to watch the Shirte Shoppe, but that crazy bat Leona would have none of it, so they just kicked out Short Marty and closed for the day. Then Two-Bit had to pack "emergency snacks," and make two last-minute bathroom stops. Finally, they were on their way.

"So where are we going again?" asked Two-Bit as they hit the open road.

"Paris."

"Which one?"

"Son of a bitch." Al pulled the Studebaker over to the side of the road.

"Let's see," said Two-Bit. "There's Paris, Texas and Paris, Tennessee. And Paris, Arkansas. Also, I think there's one in Wisconsin, Idaho, Missouri, Illinois... oh, and ain't there one in France or somewhere over thataway?"

Al lowered his head and let it hit the steering wheel. A full tank of gas was pointless if they had to cross the Atlantic. "Why didn't you say something earlier?"

"Well I tried, but you said there weren't no time for superfluidous questions." Two-Bit took a snack out of his bag. "I probably shouldn't eat this yet, especially if we gotta go all the way to France, but I'm hungry." He tucked into his ham and butter sandwich, getting crumbs all over the front seat of the Studebaker.

Even though he had told his cousin a million times no eating in the car, Al just didn't have it in him to get mad this time.

They drove back to town in silence and opened the Shirte Shoppe back up. Al sat in the corner of the store, thinking about Twyla and her long, lovely nose and fiery red hair.

A woman came into the shop and browsed, finally selecting a men's T-shirt on which Two-Bit had painted the word SHIRT.

"One of my best sellers!" Two-Bit assured the woman.

Al rolled his eyes and went back to daydreaming about Twyla. It was possible he fell asleep for a while, because when he looked around again, the woman was gone but there were several other customers browsing in the shop.

"I don't understand why you ever fired her in the first place," Al said to his cousin.

"Twyla was a crap employee," explained Two-Bit.

"It's a complex job; maybe she just needed more time to learn."

Two-Bit put his hands on his hips and huffed once. "Look around you. I sell shirts. It's not rocket surgery, Al."

"Well, still." Twyla had been a nice addition to the Shirte Shoppe. In her short stint as a shopgirl, she'd brightened the place up. He missed her presence. Her pleasant indifference had made it more fun hanging out at a shop that sold nothing but shirts. What if getting fired from the Shirte Shoppe was the reason she'd fallen on hard times, and had ended up owing money to The Skink? He'd never forgive Two-Bit.

He just knew he had a special connection with her, and he couldn't bear the thought that she was out there somewhere and needed his help. He'd do anything to get her back. Suddenly he had an idea.

Two-Bit was busy helping a customer, but Al didn't care. "Hey, Bill," he said. "Isn't there a private eye here in town? I thought you said there was one."

"There is," said Two-Bit's customer. "And it's me."

Al looked the customer over, and on closer inspection he realized he'd seen the guy around town before. "Oh yeah?"

"Yeah," said the dark-haired man. He pulled his wallet from the pocket of his trench coat and as he did so, Al swore he caught sight of a gat in a shoulder holster. The man handed Al a card which read: *Mark Ellison, Detective. If you need the scoop, I'll get the poop.*

Al inspected Mark more closely. The shifty look in his dark eyes, the fedora pulled down at an angle, the nondescript coat...

legit. "You might want to reconsider your tagline," Al suggested, holding up the calling card.

Ellison shrugged. "What kind of problem you got?"

"He's got a missing broad problem," explained Two-Bit.

Ellison nodded and made a sound indicating he knew this type of problem all too well. "Uh-huh," he said.

"I'm lucky; I know where my broad is," said Two-Bit.

"Oh yeah?" Ellison tilted his head at him.

"Yeah! She's right there." Two-Bit pointed out the shop window at a 1941 Buick Super pulling up to park right out front. He waddled out to meet his broad.

Al and Ellison watched as the town busybody, Leona Tisdale, clambered out of the Buick in time for Two-Bit to plant one on her, right there in broad daylight. Al winced, thinking it was something that he really hadn't needed to see. Apparently, Ellison felt the same way because he let out a low, "Yuck."

Al was intrigued at the coincidence of meeting a private detective right when he needed one. He figured it must be a sign. "What's your price?" he asked.

"Five bucks a day, plus expenses."

"Three," countered Al.

"Five."

"Four, plus eggs from my chickens."

"Done."

And just like that, Al had a detective on the case. He was sure to find his Twyla soon. He just hoped it wouldn't be too late.

Every night, Al went to the Aces and Deuces club, hoping to pick up some information on his girl. He would play in the band for a few hours and when he wasn't on stage, he was asking around about her. So far, that detective Ellison had come up with nothing. On Friday night, the third day after Twyla's disappearance, The Skink came into the club. Al was behind his drums when he saw the man enter with his entourage, and the hair on the back of his neck stood on end. No Twyla.

When his set was over, he stalked over to The Skink's table. "How was Paris?" he asked.

"Good, good. Always nice this time of year," said The Skink in a voice that was even scalier than his name.

Al didn't have patience for small talk. "Where is she?" he demanded.

"I don't know nothin' about what you're talking about," said The Skink.

"Bull-butts!" yelled Al. "Where is she!"

"How would I know? Look, buddy, why don't you just mind your own beeswax? Don't you got some drums to pound or something?"

Al felt a hand on his shoulder. "Just lighten up, Al," said Ellison, leading him away from the table and over to the bar, where he had two bottles of sarsaparilla waiting for them.

"How can I lighten up? I got nothing. And you—you got nothing!" Al poked Ellison in the chest with one long index finger. He picked up his sarsaparilla, looked at the bottle, and slammed it back down on the counter. "Who even drinks this anymore?"

"For your information," said Ellison in a grouchy tone, "the sarsaparilla industry is alive and well. And it's good for you, so just shut up and drink it."

Al huffed once, but then picked up the bottle again, this time taking a tentative sip. "Hey now, that's pretty good!" He downed the bottle.

"See!" said Ellison. "Oh, and I just so happen to have some information for you."

"Oh yeah? Really? That's great!" Al's night was getting better and better.

"Yeah."

Al opened his mouth to speak but got interrupted by a third party. "Does it have anything to do with Paris?"

Al turned his head to see Two-Bit standing next to them. He was looking at Ellison, who was looking confused. "No," the detective said.

"What, then?" Al would lose his cool if he had to wait for the scoop—or was it the poop?—much longer.

"Al," said Rocko, butting in. "There's something I gotta tell you."

"Come on, Mummy, back on stage!" The horn player for Al's band grabbed him by the arm and dragged him back to his drums. For the love of Pete, thought Al. What was happening? All he wanted to do was find his true love. Things were getting complicated. He counted the band in, and their last set was smoking hot.

The next day, Al picked up Two-Bit from his house and they drove to the Bull's-Eye General Store. Two-Bit liked checking out the clearance items at least once a week, and Al needed some shaving supplies. Two-Bit had insisted on keeping his cousin company on account of he determined Al shouldn't be alone.

The Bull's-Eye was a giant store; much larger than any other shop within a fifty-mile radius. "This place has everything!" marveled Two-Bit as they walked in the door.

"Just stick with me this time, so you don't get lost again," griped Al. "Last time it took me forty minutes to find you."

"I keep telling you, all you have to do is look for the cookies."

"Jeezus, Bill."

"No, cookies!" yelled Two-Bit.

They wandered down the book and magazine aisle, looking

at all the pulp fiction. Al figured he'd get something to help keep his mind occupied. "I just can't believe Ellison disappeared last night without a word," he grumbled as he picked up a Raymond Chandler paperback.

"Yeah, it was strange. He just said something about meeting Bigfoot, or going to look for Bigfoot, or something like that. Or did he say, 'old lady'? I don't remember." Two-Bit eyed a magazine called *Oprah*. "This looks interesting!" He tucked it under his arm.

"He said he had something to tell me, though."

"What did Rocko want to tell you?"

"When my set was done, I couldn't find him nowhere."

"That explains your Mr. Grumpy-pants mood," chided Two-Bit.

"Go jump in a lake."

They rounded the corner of the aisle. "I'm gonna go check the clearance rack," said Two-Bit.

"Okay," said Al, who turned in the other direction in search of the men's grooming aisle. He got sidetracked by a display of locally made sarsaparilla and picked up a six-pack to go with his book. As he got to sheets and towels, he stopped dead in his tracks and his mouth fell open. Right there, looking at some washcloths, was Twyla.

"Twyla!" he yelled, practically running over to her.

She looked up and her green eyes glinted at him, but they seemed to show no sign of recognition. Her face was unreadable as she watched him lumber over. She eyed him head to toe. "Do I know you?"

"It's me, Al! Al the Mummy! From the club?"

"Which club?"

"Uh, the Aces and Deuces? The one you were abducted from the other night."

She shifted her weight to one foot and stuck out her boyish

hip, causing Al to get goosebumps. "Look, mister, I don't know what you're talkin' about."

"Are you okay? Did they hurt you? How did you escape?"

"Are you nuts or something?" She looked around nervously, like she might start yelling for help.

"Don't you owe money to The Skink? He kidnapped you...?" Al's brain hamster was sending the message that it might be running on the wrong wheel.

Twyla laughed, but her face still showed no emotion. "You're cute," she said. "But you're crazy."

Al's arms went limp. The book and the sarsaparilla crashed to the floor.

"*Cleanup on aisle seven!*" yelled a voice in the distance.

"I did owe The Skink money," said Twyla, not paying attention to the pile of broken glass and the spreading sarsaparilla puddle on the floor. "I owed him a buck for losing a couple a games of go fish. But I paid him when I got my paycheck the next day."

It was then that Al noticed she was wearing a name tag that said *Twyla,* pinned to her red dress. "You work here?"

"Yeah! Just a few days a week."

"So..." Al was still slow to catch on. "You didn't get kidnapped."

"Well, ain't that just the dumbest thing I heard all day!" she said, inspecting the cuticles on her left hand.

He might have been slow to catch on, but he also wasn't quick to give up. It was time, he could feel it. Time for his big move. "Could I take you out on a date sometime?" he asked her. "You know, like to the pictures or something."

"Well, Mumsy," she said, shooting him a totally impassive, unreadable look. "No."

If Al had been carrying anything else, it would have dropped to the floor too.

"Oh hey, I gotta go. See ya round, Mumsy!" She skipped off

down the main aisle. Al looked up from the floor in time to see her run straight into the arms of Danny Cadence, local millionaire playboy. Bested by a blonder, richer, and younger man, thought Al. He sighed, and went off in search of shaving cream, forgetting about the soaked book and spilled sarsaparilla.

"These flowers are great, Al!" Rocko beamed from ear to ear as he pointed to an arrangement of chrysanthemums and daisies that sat at the end of the bar.

Al and Two-Bit had gone over to the Aces and Deuces after having dinner at Stacy's Joint. It was too early for the regular crowd to come in, but they went there to kill time and have a sarsaparilla.

"Yeah, whatever," snapped Al. He joined Ellison, who was already sitting at the bar. "Your information was worthless, you phony!"

Rocko and Ellison looked at him, expressionless. "To whom are you referring?" Ellison finally asked.

Al spent about two seconds feeling stupid for not having made that clear before yelling, "Both a yous!"

"Mum, calm down, buddy," said Two-Bit in a soothing tone. He patted his cousin's shoulder. "No point getting yourself worked up. Remember what the doc told you."

"All of you can just go jump in a lake," muttered Al. He turned to Ellison. "I'm not paying you, you pooper scooper!"

"Al, I do have some poop for you," said Ellison. "Just calm down, okay?" He looked at Rocko and motioned for him to bring Al a drink. "Make it something strong," he said.

Rocko looked apprehensive but did as Ellison instructed and brought Al a glass of water. With lime. "Al, there's something I gotta tell you," he said.

"No, me first." Ellison glared at Rocko.

"Just someone say something," groaned Al, reaching for his glass.

"Twyla wasn't abducted," said Ellison.

"Tell me something I don't know, you hack!"

"The car that drove by the club the other night was sending a warning to your pal Rocko here."

Al and Ellison turned their gazes to Rocko behind the bar, whose eyes seemed to get bigger as his stature got smaller.

"These peanuts are good!" said Two-Bit, plunging his fingers into the bowl on the bar.

The room was silent, except for the sound of Two-Bit scarfing peanuts.

"I..." Rocko began.

"Spill it," growled Al.

"Rocko owes The Skink," explained Ellison. "Or should I say, Rocko owes The Skink's flower shop. He owes two grand in unpaid florist bills. The Skink don't like it when his flower shop isn't making money."

"So The Skink sent a couple of his henchmen?" asked Two-Bit, his mouth full of peanuts.

"Nah," said Ellison. "That was the florist. Used to run a flower shop and numbers game in Queens." He took a few peanuts. "The guy's got skills."

Al clenched his jaw as he tried to put the pieces together. "So it had nothing to do with Twyla?" He glared at Rocko. "Why did you say those thugs in the car took her?"

"I just said the first thing that came into my head," admitted Rocko.

Everyone was quiet for a beat. Rocko slipped a finger under his collar, trying to loosen it. "Come on, Mummy," he continued. "It's not cool to owe two grand to a florist. It's way better for the credibility of the club to have the occasional abduction on account of gambling debts."

"That's true," agreed Two-Bit. "Gives you a tougher rep."

"But there were dames in the back of the car," said Al, thinking back to that night. "With big hats... oh." They hadn't been dames. They had been two fancy floral arrangements seat-belted into the back of the car.

"So, telling me they took my sweetie was your way of covering up your flower habit?" asked Al. "And then you con me outta six weeks of more flowers."

"Excuse me," said Two-Bit, who walked around the bar and pulled a giant sack of peanuts out from under it.

"I ain't proud of myself," admitted Rocko. "But they smell so nice."

Al sneezed and suddenly a horrible beeping noise started sounding from somewhere in the club. "What the—"

Al opened his eyes slowly, the beeping noise still screeching away. Only he wasn't in the Aces and Deuces Club. He was in his own bed, in his own house, and the new alarm clock he'd bought at Target the week before on a shopping trip with Bill was going off on the nightstand. He reached over to turn it off, knocking his Raymond Chandler novel onto the floor. He sighed. It was time to get up.

"That is the absolute last time I let Bill convince me to split a large spicy anchovy pizza and a twelve-pack of sarsaparilla after midnight," he moaned.

SQUIRREL TALES
I SQUIRREL YOU.

Callan Branch was the Sheriff of Logan County. His office was in Guthrie, a quaint and quirky small town which he regarded with equal parts fondness, frustration, and loyalty. Well, actually it was equal parts fondness, frustration, loyalty, and vexation, but the exact math wasn't important.

Sheriff Branch was raised in a little community in Texas, so he was familiar with the ebb and flow of small-town life. He was also well versed in its oddities, and the sometimes baffling collisions between the old and young at heart, progressive and conservative ideologies, and intellectual pursuits with those of a more industrial nature. He had spent time in Denver when he was a younger man, where he familiarized himself with the pros and cons of big city living. In time, he decided he preferred the proclivities associated with a smaller town, and had been quite happy to settle in Guthrie.

So, it was safe to say that if he hadn't literally "seen it all," he'd come pretty damn close. Even so, he wasn't quite prepared for his most recent case.

It all started on a Tuesday morning in early February. Callan was getting his monthly haircut at Craddick's barbershop when one of his deputies, Mingus Moore, came in and took the chair next to him. They looked at each other in the mirror.

"I'm guessing you're not here for a haircut," said the sheriff as Mr. Craddick continued snipping.

Mingus sighed. "Dorcas Jones got drunk and tried to do her laundry in the greeting card aisle of Walgreens again."

Since this happened on a fairly regular basis (the only part of the story that changed on occasion was which aisle she chose), Callan knew this couldn't be the only reason his deputy had made an appearance. He continued watching Mingus in the mirror.

"Also, that bookstore lady called in," Mingus said, now inspecting his cuticles.

Callan would have sat up taller at this, but knew if he did, it might prove disastrous to his 'do. Ol' Craddick was already getting a little unsteady as it was. He waited patiently for Mingus to continue but was getting irked; he knew the man was intentionally drawing this out. But he could wait. "Okay," he said.

Another pause.

"Well, she did." Mingus swung his gaze back up to the mirror.

Callan noticed his deputy was trying not to smile. Well, hell. He had been trying to hide the fact that he was mildly interested in the lady who owned the new bookstore; perhaps he had not been as stealthy about it as he'd hoped. His deputies were sharp guys and it was just plain fact that most men weren't all that subtle when they liked a woman, no matter how much yoga or meditation training they'd had. He silently counted to three while taking a deep breath, then exhaled for a count of six. An old yoga trick he'd learned back in the day. "For god's sake, Moore, spit it out."

The deputy was losing his battle with keeping a straight face now. "She called in this morning. We all thought you should take it."

Craddick's eyebrows raised, but he continued silently cutting Callan's hair.

"You need to be more specific," said the sheriff.

"We, uh...Oh heck, Cal. We just figured you could check it out."

Callan was secretly pleased at this development, but there was no way he'd admit it. "Fine," he said with the most convincingly annoyed tone he could muster. "I'll head over that way shortly."

The two men looked at each other in the mirror again, silently closing out the conversation. Mingus got up from the barber chair and sauntered out the door.

"He needs a haircut," said Craddick.

The Book Store was not too far from Craddick's, so Callan decided to walk. It was a cold day with a stiff breeze, but he didn't mind. He took long strides toward the shop and was surprised by a strange feeling that grew in his gut as he got closer. Right before he got to the store, he recognized it as nervousness. Drawing once again from his meditation practice, he observed the sensation, then let it go with an exhale before opening the door and walking inside.

As his eyes adjusted to the dim light, he looked around the front of the shop. It was cozy, tidy, and very inviting. Kind of like the owner herself, he reflected. He rolled his eyes at his own failed attempt at metaphorical artistry.

A second later, the purveyor of the shop, Beverley Green, appeared from somewhere in the back of the store. She smiled at him, and suddenly the world seemed like a better place.

"Hi, sheriff," Beverley said.

"Hello, Beverley," said the sheriff. He'd been trying for an even tone, but his voice rose when he said her name. He cleared this throat and tried again. "I heard you called in to the station this morning."

"Yeah, about that…"

Her look became thoughtful, and he became concerned. "Are you okay?"

She walked around the cashwrap and searched for something behind the counter. "Oh sure, it's just that, well, I found this in front of the door when I came to work this morning." She held out a brown paper lunch bag.

Callan took the bag. He was apprehensive but didn't want to show it as he slowly opened it and peered inside. All he saw was something that looked like a long-haired pipe cleaner.

"I… I think it's a squirrel tail," she said.

Oh no. Of all the things it could have been, he hadn't been prepared for this. *Think quick.* How was he going to handle this? A delay tactic seemed well-placed here. "A squirrel tail."

"A squirrel tail, yes. I mean, at least I think so. Don't you?"

She walked back around the counter toward him and put her hands in her back pockets, shoulders rising up toward her ears. Some complimentary words came to the sheriff's mind. He peered in the bag again. He knew full well it was a squirrel tail. "Maybe."

Callan closed the bag back up and looked at her, watching for any sign of a favorable emotion, but he saw nothing but confusion about having been served with a dried squirrel tail. Their eyes met and they held each other's gaze.

"What's it mean?" she asked.

"I don't think it means much of anything," the sheriff lied, apparently having just decided how he would handle it. "There's an antique shop a few doors down," he pointed out.

"And another across the street. It's possible someone may have dropped it when bringing in some estate sale boxes."

"It seemed like it was placed so deliberately though," she said, looking confused again. "Someone had rested it upright against the door. Butt-side down. And also there was a little flower."

He looked in the bag again for the flower but didn't see one.

"I threw it out," Beverley confessed. "I wouldn't have kept *that* thing, but I thought maybe it would be evidence or something."

Callan rolled the bag closed even tighter. "Well, let me hold onto this for you. I'm sure it's just something from one of the shops. Or a demented litterbug." He cringed inwardly. *Lame.*

"Okay," she said. "Well, I feel better now that you've checked it out. I can throw it away for you, if you want." She reached for the bag.

"I'll take care of it."

"Okay, thanks."

They stood in the front of the store. His feet didn't feel like moving. He was about to ask her something, but they heard the front door open, and in walked Bill Turner.

"Oh, hi!" yelled Bill. He looked at Beverley, then at the sheriff. His smile turned to a look of concern. "Is Beverley getting arrested?" he asked.

"No, Bill." Callan took this as his cue to leave. He looked at Beverley, then adjusted his hat. "You let me know if you need anything else," he said.

"I will," she said.

He nodded and made his way to the door. He heard Bill talking to Beverley.

"He looked weird," Bill said. "Did you do something bad?"

"Not that I know of," she said. That was the last thing Callan heard her say before he left.

Callan needed to think. And he needed something strong to drink in order to accomplish said thinking. He made his way to Hoboken, the newfangled coffee house all the kids were talking about. He'd seen Beverley go there a few times, and he wanted to see what all the fuss was, so he asked the coffee making guy—barista, was it?—what he should get. The barista asked him if he liked sugary drinks and he said absolutely not, and what he got in response was nothing less than spectacular. A cortado, it was called. Four ounces of equal parts espresso and steamed milk. He decided then and there he was a cortado man. And that he wouldn't tell anyone at work.

He sat in the café, ostensibly to people watch, but really to think about the morning's development. It wasn't much fun to people watch when wearing his sheriff's uniform; folks were always tentative and well-behaved. It was boring. Anyway. Beverley had received a squirrel tail. This was bad.

He thought back to when he got his first squirrel tail. It was many years ago, maybe the first year he'd moved to Guthrie. And it was a morning not unlike this one; a crisp, early February day. The tail had been left on the doorstep of the house he'd just bought. It was stiff as a board, straight and true, and the fluffy fur had a black stripe down the center. There was a note attached. It had been from Leona Tisdale, town matriarch and supreme busybody. Later the same day he'd gotten another one, from a teacher at the local elementary school whom he had helped one late night when she'd gotten a flat tire on one of the back roads. He'd gotten two more that same afternoon, both from married women. He had spent the entire day letting women down easy. Leona had been the most difficult; she wouldn't take no for an answer, no matter how hard he tried to get the message across that he wasn't interested. But that was a story for another day.

And now Beverly had gotten a squirrel tail of her own.

Who gave it to her? Apparently, it had no note attached. Should he tell her about the town tradition? If he didn't, she would continue to think there was some weirdo out there dumping squirrel tails on doorsteps. If he did tell her, she would know there were weirdos all over town dumping squirrel tails on doorsteps. Plus, this meant he had competition for her affections. He didn't want that, but he was certainly not going to dump a squirrel tail at her house himself. She was too classy for this small-town nonsense.

After that day those many years ago when he'd gotten four tails in one day (seven the next year, and ten the year after that, but not that he would brag about it or anything), he set about finding out what the hell it meant. It turned out that it was some bizarre courting tradition, harking back to Guthrie's territorial days. One of the town's first residents, a Mr. Herbert Klunkhammer, had a penchant for shooting squirrels who were always trying to eat the food he put out for the birds who were starting to migrate back through the area that time of year. Klunkhammer would shoot as many damn squirrels as he could and cut off their tails as trophies to celebrate his accomplishments. He also happened to be looking for a wife, and legend had it that he presented a giant box of the furry charms to his prospective bride's father as an offering of goodwill. It worked, and soon young men throughout the area were giving their sweeties squirrel tails as a sign of affection on the second Tuesday of every February. Kind of a Guthrie-style Valentine's warm-up. And to this day, some of the old-schoolers still handed out the fluffy gifts as tokens of love.

Maybe, Callan thought, if he didn't say anything to Beverley, the whole thing would blow over, and she'd never know it was a sign of affection from an admirer. Then once all this was forgotten, perhaps he could...

His cell phone rang. He pulled it out of his coat pocket. "Branch," he said gruffly.

"It's me, Beverley."

Be cool, Branch. "Hello, Beverley. What can I do for you?" His voice rose on the last word again.

"Well, I hate to bother you, but Deputy Moore gave me your number."

"Of course he did."

"What?"

"Sorry. What is it?"

"I got another squirrel tail. Only this one is... different."

"I'll be right there." He ended the call and left the coffee shop to drive back to the bookstore.

When he got there, she was waiting for him with another lunch bag.

"I don't know what to do with this," she said, holding the bag out to him.

He reached in to pull the second tail out and placed it on top of the bag on the counter. This one was shaped into a question mark, and had a small, white notecard attached to the non-butt end. He looked at her, and she nodded. He opened the card to find it contained a poem:

Roses are red,
Violets are blue,
Another squirrel lost a tail,
Cuz I'm real sweet on you.

Callan closed the card and sighed. This really wasn't good. He couldn't tell who it was from, but whoever it was, they were upping their game with fancy romantic country poetry. Now he had two competitors. It just kept getting worse. He was going to have to tell her. Maybe.

"Hmm," he said.

"I'm starting to get a little freaked out." Beverley was pacing around a table of new release fiction.

"Well now, there's no need for that."

"Umm, I think there is," she said. "I mean, this is getting downright weird."

"What's weird?" said a woman's voice from the front door. Kelly Passicheck, local attorney and Beverley's best friend, walked into the shop.

"Someone is terrorizing me with squirrel tails and creepy poetry," said Beverley.

"You mean—" Kelly stopped talking when the sheriff cleared his throat loudly and shot her a deadly glance.

"What?" asked Beverley.

Kelly looked at him again, and he gave his head the slightest shake. "Nothing," she said.

"Let me take this to the office and have my boys look it over," Callan said, putting the tail and the note back into the bag. "Meantime, don't worry about it, okay?"

She looked at Kelly, who simply nodded. "Okay," she said tentatively.

"Kelly, can I talk to you for a second? Got a question about an upcoming hearing." He nodded to Beverley and left the shop with Kelly, who hadn't said another word, as instructed.

When they got outside, she started pelting him with questions. "Why haven't you told her? How many has she gotten? She really doesn't know? Who are they from?"

He hustled her down the street a ways. "Dammit, Kelly, would you keep it down?"

"What is going on?" Kelly stopped walking and scowled at him.

He didn't say anything.

"Oh, I get it," she said.

"I don't know who they're from." He shifted his weight from one foot to the other, his long frame pitching to his left. "I..."

"You like Beverley." Kelly smiled and raised her eyebrows.

"For god's sake, Kelly, this isn't the third grade."

"Oh yeah?"

"Look, just tell her it's nothing. I'm going to see if I can find out who these are from and tell them to knock it off before we lose the best thing that's come into this town since..."

"Since what?" Kelly giggled.

"I don't know. Just do it, okay?"

"You owe me," said Kelly.

"I know."

Callan went back to the Sheriff's Department and made straight for his office, where he shut his door and placed the two paper bags on his desk. It was right before lunch; the day was still young. He recalled the year he'd gotten a total of twelve squirrel tails. Three of them from the same woman. It was someone he'd met on match.com and they'd gone on a few dates, but he had put an end to their relationship when she admitted she never read fiction and disliked baseball. Nonetheless, she left him three tails on that Super Tuesday. To no avail, as his affections could not be bought, and not liking baseball was a deal breaker.

He needed to find out who was leaving the gifts for Beverley. Who would leave her a flower, and write her poetry? A few people came to mind. One was Danny Cadence, whom he knew for a fact had a thing for her. Another was Mark Ellison, her managing editor at the Guthrie *Ledger*. But really, it could have been just about anyone.

He never got a chance to think about it further, however, because another call came in.

His assistant Ruby cracked the door open. "Hey, Boss," she called softly.

This time, Beverley had made the call from her home. Callan drove the short distance to her house, where she was waiting for him in the driveway.

"This is the last straw," she said, hands on hips. She nodded at the front door of her house.

Be cool, Branch. "Wait here," he said, walking toward the house with one hand on his gun and the other adjusting his hat. He opened the door and walked in. The living room looked like a convenience store had collided with a taxidermist's workshop.

"I kind of freaked out," said Beverly, who was now standing behind him in the doorway.

"Understandable," Callan said.

There was an empty shipping box lying on its side in the middle of the room. And spread out all over the floor were about two dozen squirrel tails. And ten Hostess Cupcakes. He was beyond feeling disappointed. Disappointment had gone on vacation and left embarrassment for the human race behind to man the fort.

"I came home for lunch, and that box was on the doorstep," she began, pointing at the now empty shipping box. "At first, I thought UPS had delivered some stuff here by mistake, instead of to the store." She sat down in a chair by the door. "I didn't give it much thought, really. So I brought it in and opened it."

He looked around the room again. She must have been so agitated that the box went flying and spewed its rodentian contents everywhere. He noticed some of the tails were dried straight as arrows, while others were in the shape of question marks. Pairs of questions marks had been tied together with something (he wasn't sure he wanted to know what had been used) to form hearts. Dang, it was creepy beyond belief, but he had to give whoever it was props for the heart-shaped ones. "Those your cupcakes?" he asked.

"They were in the box. With the, uh, things."

Callan inspected the box the items had been delivered in. He checked the label. The box had been delivered to one Mrs. Minnifred Higgenbotham, who lived north of town on East

County Road 76. The delivery service label indicated it had been delivered by Airborne Express. In 1987.

He looked at Beverley and realized she was shaking. And this made him feel worse. Here he had been concerned with protecting territory that wasn't even his in the first place, and he hadn't once stopped to think about what this was doing to her. Embarrassment for the human race went hitchhiking and got picked up by remorse.

It was time to come clean.

"I think I can clear this up for you," he said. "But first, come with me and let's get you something to drink." She was too shaken up to argue, so he led her from the house and to his SUV.

He drove her to the newest hipster brewery and ordered them both lagers. He sat her down in a booth and took the seat across from her.

She sat and watched him, speechless. He didn't know her very well, but he was familiar enough with her personality to know she was usually talking about *something*. He liked that about her; she was always good at talking to people, no matter who they were. Something that he found difficult to do. He had managed it well enough to be elected Sheriff, but it had always been a struggle. And now she was most obviously out of sorts. He hoped he could make her feel better.

A bearded hipster brewer brought them their lagers, and Callan took a long drink before speaking. "Many years ago, a strange tradition began here in Guthrie," he began. "It doesn't really have a name, but most people who have lived here long enough know about it, and while not everyone participates, some old-timers still do."

Beverley took a drink from her beer and leaned forward in

the booth, her chin resting in her hands. Callan wished she were sitting across from him at a hipster brewery, giving him that look for a reason other than having been inundated with dead animal parts.

He took a deep breath, and proceeded to tell her the story of Herbert Klunkhammer, and how his drunken pastime resulted in a holiday of sorts. As he spoke and she finished her beer, her color started to come back a little. But by the time he was done with the story, she had gone pale again.

"So you mean to tell me," she said, "that people are out there killing squirrels to give as Valentines."

"Well..."

"Son of a bitch. I knew this place was too good to be true."

"Mostly, they get reused from year to year. And on the bright side, some of the younger people who know about the, uh, festivities, insist on using faux squirrel tails. Made from natural, sustainably farmed materials. That are fair trade certified. And non-GMO."

"But who gave me an entire box of *real* ones? That's just nuts."

Before answering, he wondered if she meant to make a pun, but figured it would be best not to inquire at this juncture.

The sheriff looked up in time to see Al and Bill Turner walk into the brewery. He let out a barely audible moan, unconsciously signaling impending doom. He didn't need to be dealing with those two right now.

"Hi, guys!" yelled Bill. They walked up to the table. "You here on a date?"

"What?" asked Beverley.

"It's squirrel tail Tuesday. You guys on a date?" Bill tried again.

"Well, crap on a cracker," said Al, looking at Sheriff Branch. "You ol' smooth operator! You beat us to her."

Callan braved a glance at Beverley, who looked like she was

about ten seconds away from losing it. He had to do something to rein in the cousins, save his own dignity, and try to keep Beverley from packing up and moving to a town where people weren't completely crazy. It was time to get this situation in hand.

"Fellas," he said, standing up to his full 6'2" height, "let me buy you a beer."

Bill's eyes lit up. Callan took them both by one arm and led them to the bar, where he instructed the hipster on duty to get them whatever they wanted. He puffed up his chest, sucked in his stomach, and went back to the table where Beverley was staring blankly at a wall covered with flare. She looked so vulnerable, he observed. *Goddammit.* He sat down and took off his hat, smoothing the hair away from his forehead.

"Here's the deal," he began. "The first present you found at the bookstore was from Al. The second one, with the poem? That was from Bill. And I hate to tell you this, but that box of tails was..."

"Let me guess," she said, looking him square in the eye.

"Yes. That's right."

"I got presents from Bigfoot."

"On the bright side, they were vegan squirrel tails."

She was quiet for a beat, then said, "Actually, that does make me feel a little better."

He sure did like this lady.

SPRING CHICKEN

LOVE IS A MANY SPLENDORED THING... AND IT COMES IN ALL SHAPES AND SIZES.

Beryl the chicken sighed pensively as she stared at her captor through the chain link fence. It was true—if she had a tin cup, she would run it along the metal fence as a loud protest of her imprisonment. All she wanted was to feel the wind beneath her wings. To experience absolute freedom, just once in her life. And most of all, she wanted a Big Love. The kind of love that would consume her and give her goose bumps. A love that was forever.

Yet it seemed what she wanted most, she was not destined to have, for there was always something standing in her way. Today, it was this chain link fence.

That same morning, Beryl had woken up late. All of her sisters were already cackling out in the yard. Even from inside the coop, she could tell it would be a glorious day full of sunshine, fluffy clouds, and a light spring breeze that carried the heady scent of possibility and adventure.

She could take it no longer and went outside to wait by the fence. After a long, dreary winter, they'd finally gotten a perfect spring day. The new, light-green leaves rustled overhead. There was hope. Nothing could go wrong on a day like this. This was the day Beryl would break out. First thing after breakfast.

Right on schedule, her human minion came to their henhouse and brought food. Oatmeal, fruit, and vegetable scraps. Not a bad morning feast, Beryl had to admit. She would miss the big meals, but they would be a small price to pay for a big adventure. After she ate her fill (and then some), she announced her intentions to her sisters.

"I'm breaking out," she declared. The others just eyed her warily. Silence.

"Anyone want to come with?"

More silence.

"Suit yourself, you chickens," Beryl scoffed. And with that, she flew the coop.

She had watched her captor open and close the prison gate many times. She knew to carefully lift the latch, push on the gate, and run like the dickens. Which she did, for about ten steps before coming up against the backyard fence. Damn and blast, she forgot about that fence. She stopped just short of slamming into it, then hung a hard left and scuttled along the edge of the yard and wouldn't you know it, the gate leading to Sweet Freedom was open! She took one look back at her sisters, who were still watching her in silence. If they were considering following, there was no indication of it. None of them moved a feather.

"Chickens!" was the last thing they heard her squawk before she disappeared into the great unknown.

Beryl ran down the driveway and when she got to the end of it, chose a right turn. She once again didn't get very far, though, because now she was distracted by a set of very fine tail feathers in the front yard of the house three doors down. The very fine tail feathers were connected to a very fine rooster who was hunting and pecking around the bottom of a large oak tree.

Her run became a trot, which became a walk, which finally

petered out to a stand-still. The rooster looked up at her, an inquisitive look in his eyes.

"How *you* doin'?" the rooster asked.

"Pretty good," said Beryl. "I just escaped."

"Sweet." The rooster looked up and down the street. "So now what?"

"I want to feel the wind beneath my wings."

"But we can't fly," the rooster pointed out.

"It's a metaphor. I'm gonna get out of this neighborhood and hit the open road."

"Wow," said the rooster. "That sounds neato. Can I come?"

"I guess."

They took off down the street, together.

Earl didn't have the heart to tell his new friend that she was heading the wrong way, if she was wanting to get out of the neighborhood. She was too cute. But if he didn't say something, they'd wind up smack dab in the middle of Division Street, and that would be bad. The situation called for some tact. He'd been a confirmed bachelor all his life, but knew enough about hens to know that tact was essential.

"Say," he said. "Let's go this way. There's a yard over here with some really good worms in it." He took the next left, making sure she followed, which she did. Then he took the next left again, until they were heading in the right direction—away from town and toward open land and dirt roads. After another minute, he aimed them at a lawn that looked like it hadn't been completely drenched in pesticides. They began scratching around and as he'd predicted, they hit paydirt.

Earl watched her as she pecked around. She was pretty hot stuff, really. Cute little waddle, attractive little wattle. A rooster could get used to having a lady like her around, he thought.

Even if she had an unusually disconcerting hint of malice in her eyes and her beak looked like it could take off a few of his body parts without much effort. He found that strangely titillating.

After they'd had a light snack of worms, a couple of crickets, and some seed-like things, they continued their journey, heading in the right direction toward the border of the neighborhood. He let her lead the way; he could tell she was a lady who wanted to be in charge, and he was okay with that. Plus this way, he had a pretty good view.

After a while, the houses thinned out and the hen slowed her pace until he caught up with her. "I'm Earl. What did you say your name was?" he asked.

"Didn't," she gave as a non-answer. She was playing coy. He liked her sass.

"Where'd you say you were from?" she asked him.

"Didn't," he answered, trying to hide a smile. Two could play this game.

She cocked her head at him, and one red-ringed eye seemed to judge him like he'd never been judged before. He began to regret his decision to be sassy. "Where are *you* from?" he asked, remembering that most everyone liked to talk about themselves.

"Back that way," Beryl said, giving her dainty head a jerk back the way they'd come. "Are we almost there?"

"Oh yeah, almost." He slowed their pace; he wasn't quite ready to get there. "What are you going to do once we get there?"

"Have an adventure, naturally," she said. She wasn't slowing down, so he thought he'd try something different.

"Ouch!" He came to a stop.

Beryl stopped too, turned, and stood there, staring at him blankly.

"Hamstring cramp," he finally said after she'd made no effort to ask what was wrong or if he was okay. Fail.

They kept going until they came to a fence, beyond which

was a large open field. On the other side of the field was the edge of a small copse of trees. Beyond that...was a mystery.

Without hesitation, Beryl stepped through the fence railings and started across the clearing.

"Wait a minute now," said Earl. She stopped and turned around again, with a look so scorching he could feel his comb start to droop. "It might not be safe out there."

Beryl laughed at him. Actually laughed. Then she ran into the field.

Earl was torn. He was a worldly rooster; he knew the dangers that lurked around each and every corner. He'd seen his share of chicken disasters and took a sad kind of pride in the fact the only reason he was still around was because he'd learned from the mistakes of others. But dang, she was cute.

He followed her into the clearing.

Beryl tore across the field. Something was drawing her toward the copse of trees. She couldn't care less whether that rooster was following her or not. She was going to have herself some adventure, come hell or high water.

After being delayed by some irresistible dirt in the center of the clearing that just begged for a scratch, Beryl and the rooster reached the tree line. She hesitated. Now that she'd made it, she wasn't sure what to do.

Just then, they heard a rustling sound coming from a particularly dense part of the wooded area. Next came a low, guttural grunt.

"Hey, we should go," whispered the rooster. What a chicken, she thought.

Of course she was scared (chicken) shitless, but she'd never admit it. Adventure was what she had wanted, and adventure was what she would have. Never mind if that adventure ate her for dinner. That's how it went sometimes. But she'd never know if she never tried.

The trees continued to rustle, until finally a huge dark figure emerged. It was hard to tell what it was exactly; the shade from the trees made it difficult to determine the edges of the shape.

As it came closer, Beryl realized the edges of the creature were blurry because it was covered in thick brownish-grey fur. It kind of looked like one of those human minions, only much, much larger. Her feathers started to stand on end. Part of her knew she should run away very fast. Another part of her craved the danger of the situation, and that part of her made her stand her ground.

She heard a soft noise behind her and cocking her head, she noticed the rooster slowly sidling his way toward a bush, into which he slowly disappeared.

Damned if she was going to hide.

The figure kept coming closer, until it stopped, towering over her. She could hear it breathing and see the whites of its eyes. Suddenly her posterior end emitted a little *ploop!* sound. It turned out she hadn't quite been scared shitless. Now she was scared shitless.

"Hi," said Beryl, raising one wing slightly in greeting.

The creature raised its large and lustrous eyebrows. "Boog," it said in reply.

She wasn't sure what to do next, but she felt her fear dissipating. "What's up?" she asked.

"Boog!"

"Come on, we should get out of here!" a faint voice whispered from the bush to her left.

Suddenly the large human-y thing bent down and reached a huge furry arm toward her. In a split-second she realized it really may have been a mistake to not run away. But it was too late now. The hairy hand came down and scooped her up before she could let out even a single squawk of protest.

Well, this was it. It had been a good life all-in-all, she reflected. At least she would die knowing she'd given it a chance and had taken some risks. No regrets. She looked down at the bush and saw the shocked face of the rooster, beak agape. "Later," she said to him as she was lifted from the ground. She shut her eyes tight and mentally prepared herself for being stuffed into the maw of a prairie monster.

"Boog," the creature said softly.

Beryl opened one eye.

She was face to face with it.

It had bad breath.

She thought about pecking its nub of a nose but thought better of it.

They continued to stare at each other. Finally the thing moved again until she was positioned in front of its shoulder. Then it let go of her so she could jump on and perch next to its right ear. She hopped on, found her footing, and didn't move again, partly out of fear and partly out of curiosity.

The thing turned and started to make its way into the trees. When she looked back the way they had come, she saw the rooster standing at the edge of the clearing, his wings drooping forlornly. She felt bad for about three seconds before turning back around and feeling the thrill of adventure overtake her as they made their way into the woods. She felt the wind beneath her wings as they walked.

Squatchie found it distracting to be walking with a chicken on his shoulder, for many reasons. The main reason was that he was hungry, and she smelled like something he wouldn't normally think twice about eating. It was all he could do to keep himself from reaching up to grab her, twisting her neck, and having her for an appetizer. But there was something preventing him from acting on those most primal of instincts. Something about *her*.

He took her back to where he'd been sleeping, and plucked her from his shoulder and set her down gently next to his prized possession: a North Face backpack he'd stolen from a hastily-abandoned campsite. He had accidentally revealed himself to a small group of campers, and in their rush to run away from him, one of them had left behind his pack. Squatchie liked to keep his "special stuff" in it—a collection of found objects that ranged from small, shiny metal disks that humans liked to cram into machines to buy things; to utensils; bits of aluminum foil; and the best stuff of all—Hostess cupcakes.

The chicken slowly began to scratch around the camp site, presumably looking for something to eat. Squatchie was pleased that she didn't immediately try to run away, like most of the friends he brought home with him. For some reason, no one liked to stay and visit. They didn't seem to understand that he was lonely out here. Being a solitary cryptid was okay most of the time, but sometimes he just needed a little company; a little contact with another living thing. When he did find a friend, he would often be forced to break one or two of their legs to keep them from running away. But it didn't look like it would be necessary this time.

His stomach grumbled, and his guest snapped her head up to watch him, her wattle swinging. They both needed to eat.

"I'll be happy to go out in search of some sustenance for our evening meal, so that we may dine together under the stars on this fine evening," he said to her, announcing his intention for her to stay put while he went foraging. She didn't reply, but seemed to understand, because she hopped onto the backpack and sat on it. Squatchie smiled and went off to search for food.

An hour later, he returned with a small raccoon for his dinner, some delectable berries for dessert, and a couple of beetles for the bird. When she hopped off the backpack to greet him, it was covered in bird poop. Gross, he thought, wondering if the stuff would come out in the wash.

They spread out their goodies and had a grand meal together, even though she ate some of his berries. She also didn't seem to be much of a conversationalist. He felt like he had to do most of the talking. She clucked a few times, but mostly just stared at him blankly. Still, it was better than being alone.

Beryl couldn't believe her luck. She had wanted adventure, and that's just what she'd gotten! Abducted by a big furry thing, taken captive and forced to eat bugs! Wait till the girls at home got a load of her.

Maybe this was even going to her Big Love.

The first night, the fur thing had given her a nest to sit on. It wasn't very comfortable (who used nylon for a nest?), but it was a lovely gesture. They had sat in the twilight eating their gruel, while he kept saying, "Boog! Boog!"

She had tried to tell him she couldn't understand a word he was saying, to no avail. When they finished eating, it lay down and tucked her under its arm, falling asleep right away. She had been too wired to sleep, excited by her first full day of adventure. And what a day it had been. Eventually she nodded off, lulled into relaxation by the rhythmic snoring that came from fur thing's face. It sounded a lot like a thunderstorm.

For the next few days, they stayed at that campsite, fur thing bringing her snacks to augment what she found around the nylon nest. While the beast was gone, she would try to tidy up the place by scratching through the dirt, making piles of leaves and eating whatever looked tasty. She would occasionally roost on the fancy nylon nest and leave him an egg or two when she could. He seemed not to know what to do with them though, because he just put them inside the nest, which had a convenient plastic zipper.

Eventually they moved locations and did it all over again. It was all great fun. In the mornings and evenings they would sit and eat together, and fur thing would just say, "Boog! Booga-boog!" a lot.

"Honestly, fur thing, I don't know what you're saying," she would try to explain, but it didn't seem to help because it never said anything else other than a series of *boogs*.

On their third move, they ended up encamped by a small river.

The first morning, they ate their breakfast in silence. It seemed like fur thing never talked to her anymore.

"Why don't you talk to me anymore?" she asked. "And it's like you don't listen to what I'm saying. I'm trying to tell you how I feel."

"Boog," it said thoughtfully.

At first, being in the woods had been exciting, dangerous. She'd felt like a rebel who had a cause, and she'd felt wanted. Now she just felt unappreciated and undesired. How could something that had started out so exciting get so boring and domestic so fast?

Also, she had to admit, she was getting tired of eating beetles and berries. Would it kill fur thing to bring her a head of lettuce one time? Or maybe a little oatmeal or something? She began to wonder if it had all been a mistake. But what could she do about it? She had no idea where she was or how to get home. And damned if she would admit to anyone that she'd been wrong. Oh heck no.

Squatchie had lost track of time. All he could hear was her incessant chatter. "Bwak!" she would say. Day and night. "Bwak

bwak!" She sounded like she was screeching, and her shrill voice had him on edge.

He couldn't understand it. Here was the first real friend he'd had since his divorce. Someone who had seemed to accept him for who he was. He didn't even have to break her legs so she wouldn't run off. She stayed with him, and that did give him some comfort.

But she began to get on his nerves. She would poop on his backpack every chance she got. She never directly answered a question, always replying with that same infernal "Bwak!" Even when he tried to ask how her day was, or how she was feeling. Nothing. It was like she was made of stone. And it was starting to get annoying.

For the first few weeks, he thought maybe it was just a matter of finding the right camp. Maybe, he thought, if he could take her someplace she really liked, she would cheer up a bit and stop squawking at him so much. But wherever they went, it was the same thing. No real communication, no heartfelt talks or emotional connection. And she kept pooping out eggs. What good were they? He had no way to poach them since he'd lost his one Calphalon pot.

He had really hoped this would be the one. That this time, he could settle down. But by the time they had reached the camp by the river, he gave up hope. It was not meant to be. He remembered why he'd gotten divorced: no matter how much he wanted the opposite to be true, he had simply been born to be a loner.

One night he couldn't sleep and stayed up to watch his feathered companion roost on the backpack. They'd stopped sleeping cuddled up together the week before. Wasn't that the sign of the end? When you stopped sleeping together? As he sat lamenting the lost intimacy, he realized he had to do something. So he came up with a plan.

The next morning at breakfast, he decided it was time.

"Look, I think you're great and everything, but this just isn't working out," he said, staring at the pile of racoon fur he'd saved in his backpack as a reminder of their first night together. Now he'd taken it out of his backpack and placed it in front of her. He grew sad at the memory of how much fun they'd had at the beginning. Those days were long gone.

"Bwak," she said.

What kind of answer was that?

"Are you even hearing me?" he asked her. The question was met by a blank stare. "Okay, that's it then." He'd given it one last chance but now knew what he must do.

It felt to Beryl like the relationship between her and her furry friend had become somewhat strained over the last few days. When they first came to stay by the river, it had *Boog-booged* at her a little more than usual, arms flapping and eyes wide. But since then, the fur thing been unusually silent. It wasn't like she could ever understand what it was saying to begin with, so that part wasn't a big deal. But it was as if it had stopped trying. The newness was gone.

The day after their last "conversation," her companion had beckoned her onto its shoulder, and they took off for another new camp. They traveled for two days before they stopped and settled in. Beryl had no idea where they were; they could be deeper into the woods, or they could have backtracked.

The days had started to melt into one another, the scenery becoming a blur of green and brown. She was tiring of scratching for bugs and berries and no matter how hard she tried to explain to her friend that she wanted cracked corn and grapes and maybe some lettuce would be nice, fur thing just didn't get it. More beetles and leaves. A few times, fur thing offered her something that was obviously people food—whatever it was had a spongy texture, was dark brown, and came wrapped in plastic. She'd tried some once, but it was cloyingly sweet and she had turned her beak up at it ever since.

The morning after they'd set up their latest camp, she made an attempt to wander a little to look for a worm instead of the regular beetle fare. But her friend made a fuss every time she tried to leave, making sure she stayed put. Her patience was already starting to wear thin, and she considered making a scene. She was about to get all up in its grill, when she heard a familiar voice.

"Hey there!"

She slowly turned and spotted Earl's head poking out from under a bush.

They both stood still, not saying anything. When he made no move to leave his semi-obvious hiding place, she finally spoke. "You can come out. Fur thing won't hurt you."

Slowly Earl emerged from the bush. "How've you been? I was sure I'd never see you again."

Beryl scratched at the ground demurely. "I've been good."

"Living that life of adventure you wanted?" Earl looked at fur thing, who sat on the ground by a really grungy-looking backpack.

"Oh yeah, sure, we've been on lots of adventures." Which wasn't a lie. When she first teamed up with her friend, every day *had* been an adventure, and she had felt like she'd finally found what she was craving. Big Love, her ride-or-die adventure partner. But then... well, adventure wasn't all it was cracked up to be, but darned if she would admit that to the rooster. She looked over at fur thing, who was scratching at a spot on its leg while watching the two chickens.

"Well," Earl sighed. "I'm glad you're all right. And that you're happy." He flapped a wing at her as a farewell and began to turn to leave.

"Wait!" Beryl squawked. Earl turned back around, waiting

for her to continue. She hadn't really thought of what she would say, but she didn't want him to leave, either. "I, uh..."

"You know," Earl said, "I passed a little vegetable garden on my way over here. Some nice-looking Romaine. Want me to show you?"

She looked once more at her protector, who was now riffling through the fur on its left arm. She walked toward it. "Look," she explained to fur thing, "we had some good times, you and me. I had fun, really I did. It's just... well, this isn't working out. We're too different; we want different things from life. I appreciate everything you've done for me, but it's time for me to move on. Rolling stone and all that."

"Boog," it said pensively. It stared at her; she stared at it. They had a moment. It may not have been the Big Love she'd been looking for, but they'd had their moments.

"Okay then, see you." She cocked her head.

"Boog," it said, raising a hand.

Beryl turned to Earl. "Let's roll."

"You'll love this garden," Earl said, leading the way back toward town. "The greens looked excellent. But I'm sure you ate like a queen out there in the woods." Beryl mumbled something that he couldn't hear. "What was that?"

"I said, you'd be surprised."

They made their way to a small house on a large patch of land, and sure enough, there was the garden. Earl finagled his way through the less-than-effective fencing and made a beeline for the lettuce rows. Beryl followed close behind.

"Wow, this is amazing," she said after they'd shared an entire patch of loose-leaf lettuce.

Earl's chest swelled with pride and he was overcome by a primal sense of having provided food for his woman. However, it didn't last long; just then they heard the low, guttural growling of a cat. "Uh oh," he said slowly. "We'd better get out of here!"

They made their way back the way they'd come, at a much faster pace since a large orange tomcat was now chasing them. The cat was larger than large—it was downright humongous, but mainly because it was overweight. It didn't seem to be moving very quickly, but why take chances with something that had claws and sharp teeth? Beryl squawked in a very unladylike manner, and it was all he could do to keep from laughing at her as they scrambled for their lives.

Somehow, they made it out of the yard and to the safety of the top of a nearby parked car. The cat must not have been all that hungry, since it didn't bother following them farther than its yard.

"Is this enough adventure for you?" Earl chuckled as they sat atop the Mazda sedan and tried to catch their breaths.

"This is not quite what I had in mind, no," said Beryl. "And I'm still hungry." She looked at him. "Where have you been staying this whole time?"

He tossed his head casually to flip his comb to one side. "Oh, you know, here and there. I just go where the wind takes me." He hoped he sounded cool and worldly. In reality, he hated living in the wild. When his owners had kicked him out for getting too fresh with the lady hens, he'd been forced to forage for food, and he lived in a constant state of danger. He missed being domestic; he missed the comfort of a coop and the simplicity of backyard living. But he really wanted to impress Beryl so he left all of that out of the conversation.

Beryl sat atop the Mazda and assessed her situation. She had escaped her human, and spent some time in the woods where, she had to admit, she did have some adventures. But roughing it had proved a little too rough. And while she really liked Earl, it didn't seem like his semi-domestic hobo foraging life was much to her liking. She hung her head when she realized it.

She missed her back yard.

"What's wrong?" Earl asked.

"I..." Could she tell him? Could she admit she'd been wrong? "I sure could go for some oatmeal and grapes right about now."

"Hmm," said Earl. "I don't think I've seen any of that lying around anywhere."

They sat in silence until finally Beryl screwed up her courage. "I know where we could get some."

"Oh yeah?"

They scrambled off the Mazda and started to make their way back to Beryl's human's house. When they hopped the back fence, there was her human minion, sitting at the table.

"Beryl!" the human yelled as she sprung out of her chair. "You're back! Oh, I'm so happy to see you!" She scooped the chicken up in her arms. Beryl looked down at Earl helplessly. So much for playing it cool.

Finally the human had enough hugging, which was good because Beryl was about thirty seconds away from pecking the lady's lips off. The human looked down at Earl, who was nervously hopping from one leg to another. "I see you've brought a... boyfriend?"

Beryl shrugged in a very noncommittal way, but hoped the human minion would let him stay. "Well," said the human, "any friend of Beryl's is a friend of mine." She opened the chicken pen and put Beryl inside, holding the door open so Earl could enter too. Then she closed the gate and Beryl heard the *click* of the lock. It was a sweet sound.

"Hey, this is pretty nice!" said Earl, looking around at their new digs. There was water and food, and eight other hens watching them with curiosity. "I could get used to this!"

"Let's get something straight," Beryl said, standing up tall. "You so much as *think* of cross-pollinating with one of those hens, and I'll make sure something much worse than a cat gets hold of you. We clear?"

"We're clear," said Earl.

"Fine then."

And with that, Beryl grabbed a snack and headed to the coop for a nap. Maybe adventures weren't as glamorous as she'd thought, and the domestic life wasn't so bad after all.

Late that night, when the other chickens were asleep and the human had turned out all the lights in the house, Beryl went out for one last sip of water. It was a warm evening, and she could tell that soon the cool spring temperatures would be changing to the heat and humidity of summer. In the darkness of the suburban landscape, she sighed. Maybe it wasn't so much that she wouldn't have her Big Love. Maybe it was more about being clear on the definition of it. Maybe having a nice guy to eat lettuce with who adored her and worshipped the ground she walked on was, in its own way, a very Big Love indeed.

She looked up at the moon, and something caught her attention out of the corner of her eye. When she turned to look toward the back gate, there was a tall, furry figure standing in the shadows. It took a step forward, into the moonlight, revealing it was her friend from the woods.

It held up one hand in a silent greeting. Beryl held up one wing. They looked at each other, and a silent knowing passed between them. The figure vanished into the darkness.

FOR JULIE

TEENAGE ANGST — GUTHRIE STYLE.

Julie had always been a good kid. She never got in trouble, always got good grades, and everyone loved her. Like, everyone, okay?

When she was little, she would play for hours in the back-yard with the family dog, Penny; a small mutt with stubby legs and the body of a sausage—which was a coincidence since sausage was also Penny's favorite snack.

Julie would play quietly with the dog, acting out scenes from movies or making up stories. Everyone would remark how well she could entertain herself. She never really understood that phrase though, because in reality she was just trying to entertain the dog. But Penny made it clear she was only there for the snacks.

Julie was always able to spend time by herself, but she also had plenty of friends. Her best friend was Kim, and they had met in kindergarten when they bonded over a mutual distrust of their teacher. Julie thought Miss Baker wasn't a fair teacher while Kim thought she was too nice. But they soon became great friends anyway.

Julie and Kim played with Penny (who now had *two* people

to give her snacks, praise be to the almighty Great Dane) and went swimming and watched movies, and did all those little kid things. When they were a few years older, they would go to the library together, and they both fell in love with reading fiction. They became bookworms and it served them well over the years at school.

And now Julie was in the last few months of her senior year of high school. She was still a good kid, still got good grades, and everyone still loved her. But she had become restless.

It had built up slowly, like a thunderstorm gathering on the horizon, at the end of her sophomore year. She watched the grey clouds begin to turn darker, and move closer, through her junior year. Then she got a boyfriend, and she began to hear rumbles of thunder rolling across the sky. They made their way toward her, rattling the windows like the bass line of a Red Hot Chili Peppers song, and then sounded overhead before moving off again into the distance.

Or maybe it all moved like waves, like the ocean. Whatever it was, she wrote it down in her journal in that way only a teenager could, and wondered if she'd look at it when she was old, like maybe when she turned thirty, and marvel at her youthful wisdom.

One morning, Julie got ready for the day and descended the stairs to grab some breakfast before her boyfriend picked her up to take her to school.

"Is there any coffee, Doris?" she asked.

"It's 'mom' to you, and no, there is no coffee." Her mother crossed her arms in front of her chest defensively.

"For you, that is," said her dad, laughing before taking a sip from his mug.

"The word 'mom' is so pedestrian," complained Julie. "Let's

just call it like it is, Doris." She stood in front of the coffeemaker, debating. "Fine, I'll just have Yurt take me by Hoboken for an oat milk latte."

"Oh my god. Paul, do you hear what she's saying?"

"I like Hoboken," said Paul.

Doris turned from her husband back to her daughter. "Julie, do you hear yourself? Pedestrian? Oat milk? *Latte?*"

Julie picked up her sack lunch off the counter and a slice of toast from a plate piled high with almost-burnt white bread. "I'm still the same me, Doris, no matter which words I choose. Listen guys, I'll be home late; I'm going to study at the library for my biology test." And with that, she sashayed out of the house and into the waiting Prius belonging to her boyfriend, Yurt Yablonski.

Paul and Doris stood shoulder to shoulder at the living room window and watched their only daughter depart.

"She's dating someone named after a tent, Paul."

"It's not like she joined a gang or anything, Doris."

"She is going to drive me crazy, Paul." She wrung her hands as she spoke, watching the empty street as if Julie were still there.

Paul patted Doris' butt lightly. "I know, dear. But she's a good kid."

Yurt Yablonski was the best-looking guy Julie had ever seen, and she couldn't believe her luck when he'd asked her out one night after a JV soccer game. He had been a junior then, like she was, and had just moved to Guthrie from Sioux City, South Dakota. They never had any classes together, but Julie noticed him the very first time he sat down at the jock table for lunch. Jocks usually weren't her type, but there was something different about Yurt, and it wasn't just the fact he was named after a tent.

"Wanna go rollerblading at the Masonic Temple tonight?" Yurt asked. He had The Smiths' *Meat Is Murder* playing on the Prius' stereo; Julie was touched he'd remembered that she liked it. It was so '80s.

"I can't. I have to study for my biology test tomorrow."

"You're so freakin' smart," said Yurt. He'd said it slowly, with reverence.

And that was why she loved him. (Wait, did she love him? Like, oh my god, probably.) He never made her feel bad for being smart or for choosing studying over socializing. On the contrary, he seemed to be in awe of her. It was a refreshing change from the kids who would make fun of her for being nerdy or whatever.

"I can still help you with your math though," she said, always willing to help.

"Cool," said Yurt.

They drove a little longer in silence, listening to Morrissey pour out all his angst through the tinny speakers. *You shut your mouth, how can you say, I go about things the wrong way...*

"I wish I could have seen them live," mused Julie. She'd seen old concert footage, like from the mid-80s, and it had looked so cool. She had been born a generation too late, she was convinced.

They pulled into a space in front of Hoboken, the local coffee joint. Yurt was staring at her. "Sorry, did you say something?" she asked.

"I said do you want the usual?"

"Yes, please."

Yurt got out of the Prius and went inside to get coffee. Hoboken was too hip for a drive-thru.

Julie went through the rest of the day in a haze. She wondered about Morrissey's words from the song. It did feel like sometimes she was going about things the wrong way, but she had no idea what the right way was. How would she ever find the right way? Maybe she needed to read more books. Or go backpacking through Thailand with Yurt after graduation. Or...

After her last class of the day (which actually meant she could leave school early because she was smart and already had more than enough credits to graduate), she made a beeline for Barb's Salon where Sascha, the one male stylist and only person in the place under sixty, had a fortuitous and unusual opening in his schedule. She showed him some pictures on Pinterest and after a short but animated debate, he got to work on her head.

The whole thing took longer than expected, but she still made it to the library to study for her test, and due to an unfortunate misunderstanding about the availability of the Scottish Rite temple for public rollerblading, Yurt found her there an hour before the library closed. It was curious though, she thought, that he texted her two times to find out where she was sitting because he hadn't been able to find her. The building wasn't all that big and she sat in their usual place. When he finally sat down next to her, she looked up from her book and smiled. But her smile quickly faded when she saw the look on his face. It was a cross between terror and absolute confusion.

"I walked by this table three times," he said. "I didn't recognize you."

"Oh, right!" she said, forgetting that she'd done her hair. She smiled again. "So what do you think?"

"It's..."

Her smile faded again. "Don't you like it?"

"Well," he said, and his voice faded off. He didn't look confused anymore, just plain terrified.

The silence was deafening and Julie's face got redder with each passing second. Her boyfriend's silence spoke volumes.

She exhaled loudly and crossed her arms across her chest. Her vision started to blur with tears.

"Give me a minute," he said, sweat breaking out on his fore-head. "It's, uh, well...it's very...blue."

"I thought you'd love it," said Julie. Now her face was expressionless, and Yurt's sheen of sweat turned into rivulets running down his temples.

"Give me a minute."

"I already gave you a minute," she said.

"You didn't let me finish. Give me a minute to collect my thoughts. It's just something I'd never expect someone like you to do, is all."

"Someone like me?"

"Well come on, how many people do you see in the honors classes who have blue hair?" It seemed like Yurt's faculty of speech was returning. "It does make a sort of statement."

Julie began putting her books in her backpack. She needed to get out of the library. She hadn't cut her hair and dyed it bright blue for him, but for some reason, she had expected him to at least like it. "And what statement is that, Yurt?"

He opened his mouth but didn't say anything. He seemed to know whatever he said next would be the wrong thing. "Can I drive you home?" he finally said.

They were silent all the way to her house; nothing but the hum of the Prius to take the edge off, and it didn't do a very good job. When he pulled up at the curb, he switched off the car and turned to her.

"I do like it," he said. "I just wasn't expecting it. It's a little pedantic these days."

"You just don't get it!" She could feel the thunderstorms building and was very close to shooting lightning bolts out her eye sockets at her boyfriend.

"I liked the old Julie just fine."

"There is no *old Julie,*" she hissed. "There is only me, and this is me today." She got out of the car but before she could slam the door, Yurt leaned over her empty seat to look up at her.

"What are you guys having for dinner?"

"Really? You insult my hairdo and then you want to eat my mom's cooking?"

Yurt's gaze dropped. "Well, yeah... I was kinda hungry."

She slammed the door with a huff.

"Pick you up tomorrow?" he asked through the open window.

Julie silently debated. She didn't really want him to drive her to school, but it was either that or she'd have to drive her parent's Studebaker. She barely had the upper body strength to steer that gigantic breadbox.

"Fine," she finally said. She turned away and marched toward the house.

She could hear the Prius silently creeping away down the street. She sighed and hung her head. She really thought Yurt would have gotten it. But he hadn't even asked why she'd done it. Well, at least it had been good practice for what came next. Step 2: The Parents.

Julie opened the front door and smelled pot roast, which made her sad since she'd gone vegetarian the year before and no longer ate pot roast. She knew her mom would have something special prepared for her while they ate their meat dinner, and she would never admit to them she missed being a carnivore on nights like this. Not because she missed eating meat, but because she missed sitting down to a meal and eating the exact same thing as her parents. Like a family, like the good old days before things got complicated. Becoming an adult was so hard sometimes, she thought. Making a stand about what you wanted for dinner.

"That you, sweetheart?" her dad's voice came from the dining room. "We waited as long as we could, but we just sat down to eat. Come on in here. Your mother made you some portobello mushroom stew."

"Okay." She put down her backpack and headed for the dining room.

"You're just in time," her mom said. She was holding a soup bowl of steaming mushroom stew, walking it to Julie's place at the table. When she looked at her daughter, the bowl hit the floor and bounced on the rug before spewing mushrooms in a truly spectacular cascade across the floor. The bowl skidded and rocked on its side, making a hollow sound on the wood planks, continuing to echo for what seemed like forever. Everyone stood frozen in place until it was quiet again.

"Oh my lord," her mother finally mumbled, reaching for something to steady herself and gripping the back of a chair.

"Hi Mom, Dad." Julie slid into her seat, not bothering to get any mushroom stew or to clean up what was on the floor. *Move slowly,* she thought. *Don't want to spook them.*

"Paul, our daughter."

Julie's dad stood up to help steady his wife but couldn't take his eyes off his daughter. "Yes dear, I see her."

"How could you *not* see her, Paul? Her hair is blue. Paul, how could you *not* see her?"

"Sit down, Doris, it's all right." Her dad put a hand on her mom's shoulder and guided her to sit.

"I can explain," said Julie. She had her Feminist Manifesto Speech #7 ready to go. The one where she would eschew double standards and explain that freedom of hair color was a win against the Patriarchy.

"Paul, did somebody say something? I just see blue hair."

Perhaps Feminist Manifesto #7 would have to wait. She picked up a fluffy white roll and took a bite, wondering if it was too soon to get another bowl of stew. Maybe she should go with

Teenage Angst Excuse #22 instead of Feminist Manifesto #7 tonight. "I'm still me, Doris, no matter what my hair color is," she said, with a mouthful of roll.

"The blue hair is talking with its mouth full of food, Paul." Her mom was staring into space as if she'd lost her sight.

Her mother was blinded to the freedoms enjoyed by the modern woman, mused Julie. It must be hard to be middle aged. "Relax, Doris," Julie said.

Her dad snapped his head toward her. "That's my line, daughter. Why don't you go get another bowl of stew that your mom made just for you and your herbivore tendencies, and eat it in the kitchen?"

Julie reached for a second roll and reluctantly got up from the table. She didn't like disappointing her parents, she never had. But this time, a line had been drawn in the shag carpet and she would not retreat from it. She would set her toe as close to that line as she could. She was going to own this blue hair, no matter who didn't like it. Even her parents and her boyfriend.

"Thanks for making me dinner, Mom," she said as she left for the kitchen. She was hard-headed but she wasn't unreasonable.

Fifteen minutes, a bowl of mushroom stew and two rolls later, her dad joined her at the kitchen table. "Why do you do these things to your mother?" he sighed, putting his head in his hands.

It was the break she needed to make her case. "But don't you see, Paul? She does it to herself!"

"No Julie, I don't see. And neither do you. You are seventeen years old. You are an exceptional child and we love you more than anything. But you are just that: a child. You will call your mother 'Mom' and I am your dad. We love you. And thanks to this," he waved his had from her head to her feet under the table, "your mother is now considering sending you to her therapist."

111

"But Paul—"

"Dad. I am your dad." He turned in his chair and took both of her hands in his. "Are you okay, kiddo?"

Before she knew what was happening, Julie was crying. She cried like a little girl. She told her dad how she was scared to go away to college in the fall. She confided that she loved Yurt and that she didn't know what she wanted to be when she grew up even though her mom thought she should be a teacher. She confessed that sometimes she missed real pot roast and she actually hated oat milk.

Her dad hugged her and listened to it all. "It's okay, Julie; all of this is normal. Humans rarely get from Point A to Point B in a straight line. There are detours and wrong turns and scenic routes. And all of it is okay. Really. You will be okay."

"Thanks, Dad."

Paul went back out to the living room as Julie cleaned her dinner dishes. When she came through on her way upstairs to go to bed, her mother was sitting on the couch with a tall glass full of ice and a brown liquid.

"I didn't know there was any iced tea," said Julie.

"There isn't," said her mother, taking a big gulp from her glass and wincing.

At school the next day, Julie spent so much time and energy explaining to people why she'd cut off half her hair and turned the remainder blue that she had almost been late for her biology test. At lunch she sat with Kim, and they ate quietly for a few moments before Kim broke the loaded silence.

"So what's with the hair?"

"You too?"

Kim laughed a slightly judgmental laugh. "Oh come on! It's so out of character for you. You can't expect me not to ask."

For the first time since she'd done it, she gave an honest answer. "I don't know. I don't know why I did it."

"This must be your rebellious teenage phase," said Kim without missing a beat.

"Have you had one of those yet?"

"Yes," answered Kim. "Only I didn't put mine on top of my head for everyone to see." Kim ever so slightly slid her gaze toward her friend.

"Do you like it?" asked Julie.

Kim scrunched her face into a frown before answering. "No, not really."

If it had been anyone else, Julie would have gotten upset. But this was Kim. Her best friend since forever. She wasn't mad, but she also couldn't find words to explain.

"What did Doris and Paul think?" Kim asked, trying not to smile.

"What do you think they thought?"

Kim laughed an even more judgmental laugh.

Right after school, Julie asked Yurt to take her for a coffee but they got into a huge fight in the Hoboken parking lot before making it inside. He had practically implied her blue hair made her look less smart and that he was disappointed by this fact. Out of stubbornness and pride, she left him there and walked the few blocks to The Book Store. How shallow to be disappointed that someone looked less smart, she mused. He should know that she wasn't any less smart, or any more of anything else. She tried not to cry as she walked but when she realized she'd left Hoboken before getting a cappuccino, she lost it.

She was downright exhausted by the time she got to work. It had already been a long day. But she loved her job and she loved her boss, so as she marched through the front door of the shop, she wiped away the last of her tears and resolved to be as chipper as possible.

Beverley nearly dropped the box she was carrying when she saw Julie's hair. "Wha..."

"I know, right? Don't you love it?" Julie flipped her new shoulder-length bob around for effect, hoping she wasn't being *too* chipper.

"Are you—is that—wha?" Beverley put her hands on her hips and looked Julie over with a critical eye. "Have your parents seen it?"

"Oh my god, yes, they have *seen* it."

Beverley still seemed skeptical. "Did a boy make you do this?"

"Yurt had nothing to do with it."

"Yurt?" Beverley's eyes went wide. "Your boyfriend is named after a tent?"

Julie rolled her eyes; her patience was wearing thin. "Look," she said pointedly. "There's nothing you can say to me that my mom didn't already tell me last night. I know it's really blue. I'm still an honor student. I'm not getting into trouble, and I'll still do a great job for you here at the store." She tried to sound confident, but she could feel her emotions welling up again. What the heck! Why was this all so hard?

"It just seems so..."

"Out of character? Well, maybe it is and maybe it isn't. Do you know what my character actually is?"

Beverley put down the box and pointed to the two chairs at the front of the store. Julie slumped down into one of them, letting her backpack fall to the floor.

"You wear Vans," she pointed out to her boss. "Not exactly age-appropriate, you know?"

"First of all," said Beverley, "Vans are timeless." She held up both hands as a gesture of awe. "It's been proven with scientific studies and everything. Second, this isn't really about the color of your hair, is it?"

Julie didn't say anything.

"I didn't think so."

Julie huffed loudly and crossed her arms.

"Oh yeah, right, I wouldn't know anything about your life." Beverley laughed. "Look, you'll figure it out. If you feel like dyeing your head blue, then do it. If you feel like dating a tent, do it. Now is the time to try things out, as long as it doesn't hurt anyone. Especially yourself."

Julie scowled at Beverley. It wasn't that her boss was wrong that made her mad, but more the fact that she was exactly right. Nothing felt normal and it was unsettling. *I am human and I need to be loved,* sang Morrissey, *just like everybody else does.*

"What a great time in your life!" Beverley went on.

"You've got to be kidding," said Julie. "My parents are mad at me, I had a huge fight with Yurt, I don't know what I want to study in the fall... I don't even know what I want for dinner."

"But that's just it! Look at how many choices you have in your life. Do you know how lucky you are? You are a good kid. Very smart! You'll figure it out, I promise. In the meantime, have a little fun." Beverly shrugged and lifted one foot so they could both get a better view of her Vans.

Strangely, this made Julie feel better. She almost laughed. It was the most sense a grown-up had made in a long time.

"Do *you* like your new hair?" Beverley asked.

Julie smiled. "Yeah, I do."

"That's the only thing that matters, then. As for Yurt, he'll come around. He's an idiot if he doesn't." Beverley looked toward the door. "Speaking of idiots..."

The door opened and in walked Yurt, with a small bouquet of flowers.

Julie walked into her house a little after seven, and she could tell from the amazing smells wafting down the hall that her mom had fixed one of her favorite meals—vegetarian taco casserole. She smiled as she put down her backpack and made her way through the house to the kitchen. Her dad was sitting at the table, drinking a beer. And next to him was Kim, with Penny sitting on her lap.

"Just in time," her dad said. "Pull up a chair."

"Smells great, Mom," said Julie, sitting down across from her dad.

"Looking good, Grandma," said Kim.

Julie smiled. She was so thankful for her best friend.

Her mom brought the casserole dish to the table and sat down across from Kim. "I hope it tastes as good as it smells." Doris stole furtive glances at Julie's hair, secretly hoping that the next time she looked, it would magically be brown again.

"I'm sorry, Mom," said Julie. She looked down at the plate of food in front of her. Beverley was right. She was lucky.

"Oh, it's all right, dear," said her mom. "I'm sorry too. I'll try to get used to...to..." She waved a hand at her daughter but didn't finish her sentence.

"Good, because I really like my blue hair. But I'm still the same kid, okay?"

Her mom paused. "Okay."

Her dad sighed heavily. "Oh, good. Now maybe we can get back to normal in this house," he said.

Julie smiled. "Yeah, we can."

"Just don't go out and get any tattoos," he joked.

"No promises, Paul."

Kim snorted and her mother dropped a plate full of vegetarian taco casserole on the floor.

THE GAMMY RAYS

KEEPING THE STREETS OF GUTHRIE SAFE SINCE 1981.

That Sheriff Branch was one tall drink of water, thought Leona as she watched him saunter across the restaurant and slide into a seat across from Beverley Green. And that Beverley Green was a no-good vixen who had him under her spell. Leona continued to gawk as the sheriff leaned over the table and said something to her, and the woman had the gall to toss her head back and laugh. Floozie.

"Earth to Leona," said Margie, glaring at Leona over the top of her rhinestone-encrusted glasses.

"What? I'm listening." Of course Leona hadn't been listening, but she'd never admit that to the old broads at the table.

"I'm calling the 525th... or is this the 528th? Well shoot! I've forgotten what number meeting this is. Anyways, I'm calling this here meeting of the Guthrie GAMMY-Rays to order," said Leslie Ann, the group's secretary. "We have a lot of business to discuss, ladies, so let's order us some burgers and get down to it."

The GAMMY part of the GAMMY-Rays stood for Grandmas Against Mayhem, Muggers, and Yobs. They were Guthrie's secret, all-female, rural vigilante justice task force. They didn't participate in much actual vigilantism, but they liked to get together and talk about the sad state of affairs in their small city. Conversation was abundant since, according to Margie, the town had gone to hell in a bucket ever since the advent of rock music.

The Rays part of their name didn't have a specific meaning; they just thought it sounded cool with the word GAMMY, when they were deciding on a name. Like "gamma ray guns," the little toys from way back in the day. "We've been zapping bad guys since before you were born," they'd say to the little kids who weren't behaving in the Super Target.

The GAMMY-Rays met every Tuesday at Stacy's Place, ostensibly to discuss organizational business, self-defense tactics, and marketing strategies. But mostly they ended up eating burgers with fries and gossiping.

Daisy gave their waitress Molly the group's official *go ahead and order* signal, which consisted of an ear-splitting wolf whistle followed by a thumbs up. Then Leona spoke. "I have something we need to talk about," she said, adjusting her hair as she gave Sheriff Branch and Beverley a quick sidelong glance.

"Oh, no you don't," griped Margie. "We all agreed last time that I would get to go first this time, so first we will talk about gettin' T-shirts."

"You always want to talk about getting T-shirts," said Leslie Ann, doodling in the margin of the club notebook. "Nobody wants your dang T-shirts."

"Did you just say that you got the squirts? Because that's a little too personal for this table," said Margie, her face scrunched into a disapproving look. She was a little hard of hearing on her best day, and completely out of the conversational loop on her worst.

"No, you deaf old bat, I said nobody wants a shirt!"

"Well, that's just too bad, Leslie Ann. We need an official T-shirt, and that's non-negotiable. For twenty years you been promising me T-shirts. Well, I ain't getting any younger; in fact I'm a hell of a lot older, so we are getting some T-shirts."

It was true that Margie had been lobbying for official shirts for years. None of the ladies were T-shirt wearing types, though —not even Margie. But she had always complained that the group wasn't legitimate without a T-shirt that displayed their name and a logo. "Like the Hell's Angels," she'd told them once. "They're real legit!"

"Now," she continued, "I've had this here design drawn up, and Bill Turner says he's got a guy what can get 'em printed for dirt cheap." She passed around color copies of a mock-up design.

Leona sighed and took a sip of her iced tea. Her boyfriend Bill was great in the sack, but she had come to realize that roughly three-quarters of what came out of his face was untrue. It wasn't that he lied on purpose, per se; he just made stuff up. Or believed what he was saying was accurate, without giving it much thought. Bless his heart though, he really was good in the sack. With any luck, his claim to get them cheap shirts was just another case of overpromising and underdelivering. Or maybe he would simply forget.

Leona looked at the drawing Margie had handed her. It wasn't half bad, actually. The words *GAMMY-RAYS* arched across the top of the shirt, and under the arc was a line drawing of one of those toy ray guns they used to have in cartoons and comics. Under the ray gun were the words, *KEEPING GUTHRIE SAFE SINCE 1981*.

Had it been that long? Leona felt old. She was in her seventies, but still thought of herself as a spring chicken. Just then she heard Beverley laugh again, and she suddenly felt unbearably old. A pang of what could only be described as jealousy tinged with a touch of regret wafted across her consciousness.

"What's the GAMMY part stand for again?" asked Daisy. At 91, she was the oldest member of their group and considered herself to be their founding member, president, spokesperson and self-defense coordinator. In reality, it was Leona who was the one who got things done, but they all let Daisy think she was in charge.

"Yeah, maybe we should put that on the shirt, you know?" said Leslie Ann. "So people know what it stands for."

"Son of a bacon bit, Leslie Ann, no one's supposed to know we even exist!" Leona's voice went up an octave and she could feel an almost manic level of frustration coming on. Normally she wouldn't think twice about using real cusswords, but Daisy meted out some rough justice when she heard any of the Gammys using foul language. "We end up going over this every damn—darn time. Margie, we can't get shirts, we're a secret organization."

Margie laid her drawing down on the tabletop. "Hmm."

They all sat in silence as Molly brought their burgers.

"Well," suggested Leslie Ann, staring at the top of her burger bun, "what if we left off all the writing and just made T-shirts with a picture of a ray gun on 'em?"

Leona wanted to smack her, but instead ate a forkful of fries.

Conversation moved on to other items on their agenda as the ladies ate their burgers and ordered dessert—a vanilla milkshake for Leona, chocolate silk pie for Margie, blackberry crumble for Leslie Ann, and a cinnamon roll for Daisy, who had diabetes but didn't give a flip on meeting day.

They revisited the suggestion to meet somewhere besides Stacy's Place (a motion which had been raised every few months since the unfortunate food fight incident of October 1992), but once again the debate ended in a stalemate. They could never decide on a suitable replacement restaurant. Leona wanted sushi at Sushi R Us, Daisy wanted to hit up Pie Universe, Margie wanted to go to Nuttin' But Nuts, and Leslie Ann was a diehard fan of the pizza over at Guy's Pizza and

Vacuum Repair. Somehow, they always agreed to keep going to Stacy's.

As always, Daisy wanted to show them her latest gun acquisition, which this time around was a new Glock. She almost pulled it out of her purse and set it on the table before Leona figured out what she was up to and strong-armed the woman into keeping the thing in her purse. Daisy had a thing for guns, and tried to treat their public meetings as a weapons show-and-tell.

"Well then, I move we have our next meeting at the shooting range, so I can show you what this baby can do!" said Daisy, patting her purse.

"You know we can't do that," snapped Leslie Ann. "Their snack bar sucks."

"Did you say it cost you fifty bucks?" asked Margie.

Leslie Ann patted her hand. "No dear, just eat your pie."

"I'm done already!" said Margie, looking predatorily at everyone else's desserts. Leona noticed she had chocolate pie filling all over her top lip, making her look more than a tiny bit like Tom Selleck. The current vampire one, not the sexy *Magnum, PI* one.

Leona checked her watch again. "Are we done with all this nonsense? It's time for our guest speaker."

Just then Sheriff Branch appeared at the head of their booth. All four ladies looked up at him adoringly and a collective sigh could be heard. "Hello, ladies," he said in a deep yet neutral voice.

"Well lookie here, it's Sheriff Sexypants!" said Daisy, who had absolutely no filter left. She didn't care what she said, who heard, or how far away they were sitting when they heard her.

Leona noticed the sheriff start to look uncomfortable, so she intervened. "Right on time, Sheriff Branch, we're ready for you." She shoved Daisy toward the wall and made room for him right next to her.

"Oh, you bet we're ready for you!" said Daisy. Her eyes were sparkly pinpoints of light in her wrinkled face.

The sheriff smiled weakly and sat as close to the edge of the bench seat as he could. It looked to Leona like his left butt cheek might have been hanging off the side. "Let's bring this butt cheek to order," said Leona.

"Did she say, butt cheek?" asked Margie.

"She sure did," said Leslie Ann. Margie nodded in agreement.

"So, um, what can I do for you ladies?" The sheriff looked at his watch.

"Thank you for coming to our meeting," said Leona. Damned if she was going to let one of these old vultures monopolize this fine man's time. "We've got some questions for you."

"Okay, shoot," he said, clasping his hands together and placing them on the tabletop.

"Shoot?" asked Daisy, reaching for her purse. Leona elbowed her. "Ooof!"

"As you know," continued Leona, "us four ladies comprise a secret vigilante group." She looked around at her friends, who nodded encouragingly.

"The Gummy Bears, right?" he asked.

Margie threw up her hands and rolled her eyes. "Jesus."

"It is the GAMMY-Rays, sheriff," explained Leslie Ann. She slid her copy of Margie's T-shirt design over to him.

"Ah, I see. Well, about that—"

Daisy held up her hand to interrupt him. "We know what you're gonna say, Sheriff Sexypants, and we're not gonna disband. No how, no way."

"You are one of the only people who know about our group," said Leona.

"About that, too—"

"That is beside the point, and not on the agenda for this meeting." Leona was aware of the fact that they were probably less of a secret than they believed, but they liked to keep up the appearance of not having an appearance. She was still not going to authorize T-shirts.

"Okay," said the sheriff.

"Anyway," said Leslie Ann, "we want you to be on our board of directors type thing, and we want to form a joint task force with the Sheriff's Department on crime in Guthrie."

"Let me get this straight—" He tried once more to speak but again didn't get very far.

"We want you to deputize us!" said Margie.

"Yeah, then maybe my new Glock will get some real action!" said Daisy. "Want to see?" she started pulling her gun out of her purse again.

"Jiminy Christmas, put that thing away!" scolded Leona, yanking Daisy's purse from her.

"Please don't tell me she's really got a Glock in there," said Sheriff Branch.

"Okay," said Leslie Ann. "Leona, don't tell him."

The sheriff rubbed a hand across his stubbled chin in dismay, causing the whole table to swoon and go silent. He quickly put both hands on his hat, which was in his lap, but still caught Leona eyeing him hungrily. "Don't you have a boyfriend now?" he asked her.

"Yeah. So?"

"Just making conversation." He looked around at the ladies.

Leslie Ann leaned in toward him and inhaled deeply. "You smell yummy. What *is* that you're wearing?"

"Dust and coffee."

"Dustin Hoffman?" asked Margie. "I gotta get me some of that for Franklin. Where'd you get it? Jeepers, must be nice to have a perfume named after you."

The sheriff opened his mouth to speak but Leona put a hand on his arm and said quietly, "Don't bother." She surreptitiously inhaled deeply. He did smell awfully nice. Too bad Bill didn't smell like that. He usually smelled like a combination of Spam and Dr Pepper.

"Hi!" Leona looked up to see Beverley Green standing in front of them. Oh, for crying out loud. The woman was everywhere.

"Hiya, Beverley!" said Daisy. "Want to see my gun?"

"Is that a euphemism?" asked Beverley.

"Did she ask if we were superhuman?" said Margie.

"Yes," said Leslie Ann. "And I told her you were made from leftover bicycle parts."

"It does kind of smell like farts," said Margie, waving her hand in front of her face.

"Uh," said Beverley, eyeing Margie, "Anyway, I just stopped by to say hello and see how the GAMMY-Rays meeting was going."

"Well, aren't you just the sweetest," said Daisy.

"You're not supposed to know this group exists," complained Leona. "Callan Branch, did you tell her?" She was starting to feel her blood pressure rising, which was never a good sign. How could he betray their top-secret club by telling that hussy about it? She had tried to be nice to Beverley on many occasions, but Leona just couldn't see what he found so appealing.

Once more, the sheriff started to say something but didn't get a chance to.

"Oh no, he didn't say a thing!" Beverley assured them. "Bill mentioned it the other day, said something about some shirts. Hey, if you guys make shirts, can I have one?"

Leona clenched her jaw so tightly it popped. She was about to break. But if she started yelling at Beverley, she risked losing the respect of Sheriff Branch, and that would just be too much to bear. She would bite her tongue for his sake. For now, anyway. And she was going to have to have another chat with Bill about what he could talk to other people about, and what was told to him in confidence. Maybe a graph and some charts would help him understand.

"We're not having shirts made, dear," Leona said with her fakest smile possible. "And our membership is closed."

"Oh, I didn't want to join, so that's okay. Well, I need to get going. You ladies be sure to stop by the bookstore soon to say hi! Jimmy the turtle misses you." Beverley looked down at the sheriff and her smile got bigger. "See you later," she said directly to him. He turned red and simply nodded.

Daisy, Margie, and Leslie Ann waved at Beverley and said their goodbyes to her as she left the restaurant.

"That Beverley is such a nice young lady," said Daisy. "Sheriff, you should tap that."

"Good grief!" exclaimed Leslie Ann. "Daisy, do you even know what that means?"

Daisy sat up straight and smiled. "Sure, isn't it like when you wanna go steady with someone? Like takin' your girl home to meet your parents."

"Is that like playing 'hide the kielbasa?'" asked Margie. "Because I've never heard it called 'meeting the parents.'"

The sheriff put his elbow on the table and his hand to his forehead.

"Well, anyways. How's about it, sheriff?" asked Leslie Ann. "We wanna be deputies."

"I'm sorry, y'all. The Logan County Sheriff's Department appreciates your concern for our city, but you know I can't deputize you," he said.

"What if we gave you one of our T-shirts?" asked Margie, pointing to the logo he was still holding. "Size extra-hunky?"

"It's tempting, but I just can't. And you know I don't officially recognize or approve of the GAMMY-Rays."

"Oh, that's just on the record," scoffed Daisy. "In real life, we know you rely on us for the well-being of the city."

"How about letting us do some ride-alongs?" asked Leona. "Or walk with your deputies in the Christmas parade?"

"Wouldn't that blow your top-secret status?" he countered.

She hadn't thought of that. Leona was so desperate to be recognized by the sheriff, she would almost be willing to give up their top-secret status. "How about if I got you a bottle of Hendricks?"

He laughed a melodious prairie cowboy laugh. "Also tempting."

Leona thought back to the previous Christmas, when he had brought her a bottle of Hendricks, got her sloshed, and convinced her not to evict Beverley from the building housing her bookstore. It had been a great night.

"You can't have it both ways, Leona. If you want your group to remain exclusive and secret, then you can't very well participate in any public events."

"He's got a point," said Daisy.

Leona frowned. He knew what he was doing, making them choose like that. He was not only cute and smelled great, but he was damn smart.

"Well," she said, "I suppose you're right. It's more important that we maintain our anonymity, so we can continue to keep this town's streets crime-free."

"Yeah, I think that would be best," said Leslie Ann.

"I've got to run," said Sheriff Branch, getting up from the table. He looked down at them and put his hat back on, pulling the brim down as a slight smile appeared on his face. "You take care, and thanks for keeping Guthrie safe." And with that, he strode out of the restaurant.

"Did he say he was starting to chafe?" asked Margie. "I hate it when that happens."

Thanks for reading! I'm currently writing the next book in this series, so if you enjoyed this tale, be sure to keep in touch so you won't miss the next Beverley Green Adventure.

Never miss a new release - follow me on BookBub! (www.bookbub.com/authors/andrea-c-neil)

Join my newsletter to keep in touch and receive extra content. Thanks again!

BOOKS BY ANDREA C. NEIL

Want to read more about Beverley and her pals? Check out the rest of
THE BEVERLEY GREEN ADVENTURES

Beverley Green: Sasquatch Hunter

Beverley Green's First Territorial Christmas

Beverley Green Finds True North

Beverley Green Comes Home

The Guthrie Short Stories, Volume One

Short on time? Try some bite-sized short stories!

Days Are Beautiful: 100 flash fiction stories

*Visit acneil.com and sign up for the Ace Writes Newsletter to stay in
the loop!*

ABOUT THE AUTHOR

Andrea is a writer, yoga teacher, and professional introvert. She balances all of this with the help of coffee, chocolate, and plenty of irony. Not to be mistaken for ironing. She doesn't do any of that.

She's part of a ridiculously creative family, and is the niece of Eleanor and Francis Coppola. They and their family have been a source of inspiration and encouragement.

Andrea's "Beverley Green Adventure" series might be best described as "GenX Chick Cozy Lit Comedy Adventure." Until BookBub creates a category for that, just know her books are filled with laughter, lightheartedness, and yes, plenty of irony. The books follow late-bloomer Beverley as she navigates new territories in her mid-40s: a new town, a new career and a newfound appreciation of nice guys.

"Days Are Beautiful" is a collection of 100 flash fiction stories, each of which are 100 words long. Written one per day during the early days of the "2020 stay at home party" (still searching for a kinder alternative to what to call it), the stories come together to form an unusual journal of an unusual year.

She lives in Tulsa, Oklahoma but was born and raised in Southern California, where she still visits regularly in non-pandemic years.

Sign up for the AceWrites newsletter at acneil.com today!

facebook.com/andreacneil

instagram.com/andreacneil

bookbub.com/authors/andrea-c-neil

goodreads.com/andreaneil

Made in the USA
Las Vegas, NV
10 November 2020

10671414R00083